Tales of Fire

Pages from my Personal Diary

Bleue Notes Publishing
PMB130
3520 Okemos Road, Ste. 6
Okemos, MI 48864
U.S.A.

www.pandorableue.com

Tales of Fire

Pages from my personal diary

Pandora Bleue

Bleue Notes

With Love To:

J, S & M for keeping me grounded, even when you didn't know that's what you were doing. To Nanc, whose unwavering friendship and relentless ass kicking was both appreciated and necessary. To Luigi, for making me laugh and for translating technical weirdish into comprehensible language and to Aphrodite for holding my hand.

Dear Reader,

After they've had their first major orgasm, every young person believes they invented sex. Every deflowered female who has had the pleasure of a truly good lover will thereafter, carry herself like Aphrodite in the flesh. There are a finite number of natural orifices on the human body. That has never changed. Skin has always been wired to react to hot and cold, caresses and pain. Given the proper attention, everyone's body awakens, blooms and bursts into white hot flames and memories that continue to reignite as long as you can remember them.

We are all sleeping cocoons of electricity until someone comes along and wakes us up.

My diary was written with a pen of fire and it has been, for years, the silent keeper of my most private life. After hearing a few of these entries, a friend encouraged me to share some with others who were searching for stories that heat the flesh and stir the juices.

I offer to you, my dear reader, tales of fire from the pages of my diary. They move, like our memories do, in random time order. Read them while you are alone. Read them aloud to your lover. If you have been inspired by the little moments you've experienced on these pages, be brave and write down your own stories with your own pen of fire.

Burning,
Pandora

Table of Contents

Introduction

While going through some of my old diaries I have had many delicious hours revisiting these moments spent close to the fire of sexual passion or standing in the center of its heat, letting it burn away reason and inhibition in its flame while I followed the impulse that arose in the moment. Some are memories as sweet as honey and others are sudden, raw and real as the sting of a whip on tender skin.

The work I have done as a photographer and writer has given me a backstage pass to real life happening. Long ago, I decided that if I was going to do this thing, to write down on paper where my hands and my body and my mind are travelling, then I need to start this honestly. There is no one who knows my body like I do. I was my first lover. I started the fire with my own hands and every time I burn again, the choice, the variable, is whether or not I want to invite anyone to share the heat.

Sexual contact is a glorious buffet of flavors and textures, colors and sizes and levels of hardness from the ultra soft tongue to the metal grip of a handcuff. Before I can say what I do like and what I don't like, I need to taste, to sample everything from a delectable wet cherry to a habanera hot meat that I can barely contain in my mouth. I need to see what it looks like from the viewpoint of the observer when a mouth meets a mound and a face strains in ecstasy. I need to burn in every way I can before I know the nature of my fire and can say, honestly, this is what I like.

No one knows my body better than I do. We women know the feel of our own breasts brushing against clothing as we walk. Our nipples stand alert when a thought or a look or a memory pings our on button sending a jolt of electricity from our crotch upward awakening the thousands of receptors ready now for touch. If we could see it, I'm sure a wave of rose and purple energy blooms at our clits, rushing over us until our pupils dilate and our breath catches. When it happens for me, my entire being shifts into high alert. My senses kick into overdrive like a leopard on a hunt. Muscles coil, eyes narrow and I'm ready for whatever comes my way.

Women know the feel of our own hands sliding, secretly down our stomachs seeking out the warm place between our legs, eager for the thrill of finding wetness; evidence of the lighting of our private fire. No one knows our bodies better than we do. In order to know our selves completely, we must learn what we crave through living our own tales of fire or by hearing someone else's so we can know what our own mind's vagina really hungers for. We need to learn what a cube of ice will do to every part of our anatomy. We need to learn what vibration can bring up and over us. We need to cum so hard that we shake our heads and howl and we even need to find a way to let someone watch us get there on our own, even if that only happens once in our lives.

Stories that touch the erotic nature of our lives give us per-mission to live, for a moment, in a private world that every woman, any age, any size, any color holds deep in the velvet folds of their mind's vagina.

When I sit in a public place with my e-reader and notice the man across the way with the chiseled jaw line, the woman brushing by with her blouse a button too open and a show of lace as appetizer, I know they have no idea that what I'm reading is making me so wet that I fear when I stand, I'll leave a puddle where I was. I want you to feel that too.

Stories like these, these tales of fire, should reach around us from behind and press up on our backs. Flames should be hovering over our skin as we move through the world and anyone looking our way should feel the heat coming off us. The tongue of these words should lick a line from the hollow of our throat up, forcing warm air into our ear with a whispered and desperate YES. Don't apologize for knowing this part of you, for the world would not go on if it never did.

I've gathered some of my own stories here to share with others, to be used as fuel for your own burn. Just as every encounter is different, so are the stories on these pages. Some may be too much for you. Some may be not enough and some will wrap around you so completely, that after reading them, you will walk around for days reliving moments for your own secret pleasure. You will only know which is which after you've lived with each one for awhile.

The names in my diary are, of course, changed to protect the not-so-innocent, but the content is very, very real.

No one knows our bodies like we do. Let me tell your mind's vagina a private little story that goes like this…

"Graze on my lips; and if those hills be dry,
stray lower, where the pleasant fountains lie."

William Shakespeare

Chapter 1

Saint Emilion, France 1996

Secret Garden

While in rural France on sabbatical to finish a book project, I spent my free time wandering the small villages and countryside. Solitude, anywhere, was a luxury for me with a print deadline to meet of October and I relished any unstructured time I could carve out of my summer days.

Back behind the little country house I had rented there was a stand of trees that bordered the vineyard one property over. I had met the middle aged couple who owned the vineyard, Jacque and Manon, early on in my stay and we had shared a few meals together. Manon and I had spoken over the garden fence a few times, but she tended to keep to herself mostly, letting me go about my work blissfully uninterrupted for the majority of the summer.

Jacque, a stoic man in his fifties, was rather distant and cold. I never saw him smile and his distracted and restless manner caused him to appear constantly angry about one thing or another. This was in such sharp contrast to the easy going and friendly way that Manon had about her. She knew all the workers at the vineyards, their spouses and children, as well as the local village residents and shopkeepers and a day never passed when she wasn't humming as she went about her work in her garden or stirring a kettle on the stove. Though she was also somewhere in her fifties, she had that lovely French woman gift of maintaining her beauty throughout her life. Her hair was still a pretty brown with just a few wisps of gray at her temples and the lines around her eyes were few and I'd guess she earned them laughing.

I didn't know the story behind the way this strange couple had met and come to be married but would ask her someday when the opportunity arose. Their grown sons had left the vineyard; one now at university in England and the other had a travel itch and was making his way around the world.

Each afternoon, I would spend a little time in a shady spot out in the tree grove. Sometimes I'd bring a bit of lunch and a blanket so I could read or take a nap. From this cozy spot, I could see down into part of the vineyard and across the gardens of our two properties. The fragrance of lavender and sweet grasses mixed in the summer air with the earthy scents that came to me on breezes. It was easy to just drift off in this perfect setting.

On one of those dreamy hot afternoons, I was stretched out and dozing beneath the canopy of leaves with a bundle of peonies I had gathered to bring into the house and set in the large green glass vase. The clinking sound of a garden tool brought my attention to the neighboring yard and I noticed Manon had come out to work in her lavish garden. Every sort of kitchen vegetable you could imagine seemed to thrive with her touch and she would hum while she knelt to pull a weed or prune a plant. Jacque would be gone for the week and I thought I should invite her to go with me to the village one evening so we could see a movie and have a meal at one of the small bistros near the center square. I made a mental note to ask her when I headed back to the house in a while.

While she worked, I noticed that one of the vineyard workers was also watching her. His back was to me so he had no idea I was there and I could easily see where his gaze was focused. It was Alain, a local man who had been learning the winemaking business at their vineyard since he was a teenager. Now in his thirties, he assisted Jacque in the fine art of pressing, blending and aging wine in their traditional oak barrels. Any true vintner will tell you they are farmers, as the tilling and pruning and care of the vine is more than 80% of their job each year. With Jacque out of town, it fell to Alain to inspect the entire acreage on foot and this was where he'd gotten to today in his rounds.

Alain was standing just outside the garden fence watching Manon as she would bend and work or kneel and gather ripened food into her basket. He watched the curve of her cotton dress with its tiny flower print and how her hair had come loose in strands that she would occasionally try to push back with a forearm as she worked. He watched the damp glisten of her tanned skin and while he watched, I saw him rub his hand over the front of his jeans on the growing bulge.

Alain was fit and tall and though he was not model handsome, there was ruggedness to his look and the confidant way he carried himself made him more attractive than most carefully manicured show princes of the city.

He had beautifully muscled arms from lifting barrels and doing the hard physical labor that filled his days and from my view, I could see his bicep flex as he moved his hand.

His lean torso and firm rear end sent a shudder through me and I thought about joining him in his voyeur game and helping with his growing problem.

A few moments later, his hand was on the garden gate and I watched as he quietly made his way to Manon. He arrived behind her just as she had stood from her work and she did not notice him there. I watched as he pressed his body up against hers and brought his hands around cupping and kneading her breasts. It startled me and I wondered if I should perhaps call for help but the moment I saw her head fall back onto his chest and the look of pleasure on her upturned face, I knew that this must be the inspiration of her humming in spite of all those years with her cold and distant husband.

He held her that way, her facing away from him as he ran his hands all over her body. Her dress, clinging already from her sweaty work, stuck to her thighs and he ran his hands up and down them paying special attention to where they met.

He reached down and lifted the back edge of her dress up to her waist and then slid her panties down exposing her slightly plump and nicely rounded ass to the garden air. Running his hands over each perfect peach and up around beneath her clothing, he could feel her naked breasts. I couldn't see his hands as he caressed her that way but from the sounds she made that floated on the breeze and up to where I was I could easily imagine the pinching of nipples and the feel of a strong man's hands sliding under to lift the weight of her breasts in his palms like plump doves.

Alain kissed her neck while he explored her and slid one hand down to find her sex. He never turned her towards him or kissed her lips; a thing I found very erotic. He loosened his pants and freed his cock which sprung out eager and rock hard. Wrapping his arms around her from behind, he criss crossed them on Manon's body; his right hand to her left breast, his left hand to her right breast. He bent his knees slightly and angled himself until his hardness found its way between her legs.

Alain held her there, lifting her slightly off the ground while she helped by straining up on tip toes to let him find her deepness. They did not speak. I would have heard them. He stood with his muscles taut and his head thrown back in ecstasy and silently ground his hips as he pumped into her over and over. They moved that way, with a motion like two Latin dancers locked together and lost in the music. I was mesmerized by the raw passion of the moment and it was a beautiful sight to behold as she moaned up to the sky; Manon and Alain in their secret garden.

Had this been going on for some time? She was twenty years older than him yet their bodies seemed to fit like puzzle pieces and the skilled way they did this cock and pussy dance told me this wasn't their first encounter. He was savagely thrusting now and her flush faced pleasure only grew as he held her there with his hands locked over her breasts and her peach fine ass rammed against his thighs. I could see her legs shaking as she tried to stay up on her toes while he thrust into her from behind.

With a lovely shutter of orgasm, they climaxed together and she dropped her hands to her knees for balance while he rested his head on her back. Alain waited there only a moment and then put his lips to her back, zipped up his pants and left the garden to finish his work in the vineyard.

I watched Manon as Alain disappeared. She smoothed her dress down while tucking her abandoned panties into her gathering basket. She stood and stretched her arms high above her head and in a moment of joy, she whirled around and I heard her laugh carry up to me.

Manon saw me then, up on the hillside and her hand flew to her mouth in surprise. I stood up from the blanket where I was and grabbing the armload of flowers I had gathered, I tossed them into the air, kissed both my hands and blew the kisses down to where she stood.

She smiled at me and I smiled back and then she made her way towards her house with her vegetables, her panties, my wind kisses and Alain's passionate offering, still hot and moist between her legs.

"A dirty book is rarely dusty"

Author Unknown

Chapter 2

Los Angeles 1974

An Intimate Dinner for Four

The gift box was left at my front door. I saw it there when I went to bring in my morning newspaper. It was silver with a red satin ribbon and no visible note. I carried it with my paper to the patio where my breakfast was waiting.

Not being a very patient person, I set the box on the table and quickly pulled open the ribbon to see what I'd gotten. Beneath the tissue was an envelope and under that was a very expensive looking white French lace bra with a demi cup that would never cover even half my breasts. The second item was a white g- string, meant to be panties I assumed, and a garter belt with matching lace. It was like a small apron with pristine white cotton strings for tying in a bow at the back. The last item in the box was a velum bag with a pair of sheer, white nylons. Benjamin wanted to play another seduction game with me and I swallowed a giggle anticipating when I was supposed to wear these and more importantly, where.

He had a vivid imagination and often made steamy phone calls instructing me to listen while he talked. I listened until I was so aroused that I insisted he pay me a visit immediately or I would grab my car keys and make the twenty mile drive to his home so he could make good on his promises. Whatever he was up to with this new fantasy, it was going to be juicy and fun.

The note simply said, *"Pandora, wear these with your grey suit, white blouse and your black high heels to work today. Dinner is 7 pm, at Vincent."* and he simply signed it, *"B"*.

I worked at a photography studio and would have no reason other than a client meeting, to wear a suit...or nylons...or four inch high heels. But that was the point. Wasn't it? He enjoyed creating situations for me where I had to wear or say or do something overtly sexual so that anyone watching had some inspiration for their fantasy jerking off sessions later.

A master of small seductive details, Benjamin knew that this outfit, at 10 am on a Wednesday, would look completely out of place and that I would be compelled to explain to co-workers that I had a date after work and wouldn't have time to change. He knew that the boys in the equipment room would be walking around with a hard on all day as my too short skirt was constantly adjusted to cover the exposed clips and the top edge of my stockings and garter belt. He also knew that in this summer heat, I would either keep my jacket over my blouse all day, or

I'd remove it exposing the bursting cleavage through my cotton shirt.

While I showered, I was trying to imagine my day if I decided to comply with his request to wear this outfit he must have seen on some bosomy babe in one of his many men's magazines. Dressing up for dinner was simple enough, but trying to perform all my regular tasks at the studio all day meant ten plus hours of awkwardness for me. For him, it was an all day form of titillation as he pictured my difficulty at staying chaste in the workplace in this get up.

I adjusted the clip on the nylons so they would lay flat on my thigh and smoothed my skirt down. I tried, again, to adjust my breasts in the demi bra so my nipples wouldn't be so visible through the white cotton blouse. It wasn't working and the lace edge seemed to catch on my now, hard nipple, lightly scratching the tip like a teasing fingernail as I moved, causing it to remain puckered. I pulled on the jacket and knew I might be roasting moving from the house to the car, in and out of air conditioning. If I was going to do this, I may as well do it right. Go big or go home, as Benjamin liked to say.

I decided to wear my glasses rather than contacts and I piled my hair up in a loose bun at the back of my neck, playing up the whole hot business woman image. Heading for the door, I saw my scarf on a coat tree and grabbed the blue silk and draped it over my neck. I laughed thinking of how women at church who had forgotten their hats, would often use a handkerchief or in desperation a Kleenex held with a bobby pin on the top of their heads as the makeshift mantilla. My scarf was going to have to serve as a barely adequate accessory to help cover my breasts and besides, it wasn't technically cheating as I had the rest of my gift on under my clothing.

About noon, I picked up my ringing phone, "Photography Department. This is Pandora. How may I help you today?" With no greeting, he spoke, "Put the phone between your legs and snap the garter so I know you're wearing it." With a mad blush on my face, I lowered the phone and grabbed the elastic of the garter lying on my left thigh. I gave it a snap. "Happy?" I asked. "Very," he said, and the line went quiet. He could make me wet with a single word.

By 6:30, I had cleared my desk and had my schedule posted for location shooting the following day and I made my way through the studio to leave. Wayne from the equipment department called out in his best Mr. Moviefone voice, "It's a heat wave in Los Angeles when Pandora comes to town."

"Thanks Wayne. Very funny."

"Tell Ben he's one lucky dog." He added.

"Will do."

At the restaurant, I saw him facing the back of the room. He was already seated and he'd chosen a table for two just off the main aisle of the dining room. Of course he would sit there. It had a larger viewing audience for whatever show I would be putting on for him and whoever else would be watching.

As I approached he rose and took my hand, leaning in for a nice kiss. "You look fantastic." He added with a voice like a finely tuned cello. He looked pretty fantastic himself in his charcoal suit and teal silk tie. It set off his blue gray eyes and the summer sun streaks in his dark blonde hair. He had been mistaken for a popular actor on occasion;

once as we stood in line at a grocery check-out together and the obviously smitten teen cashier had asked if that was who he was. I'd given her a wink and patted his tight ass and if jealous looks could kill me, I'd be dead.

When he settled back into his chair, Benjamin reached into his jacket pocket and brought out a small notebook like correspondents use for field notes. Reaching in again, he removed his Mont Blanc pen and set it on the note-book. I thought we would be talking, but it seemed that this was going to be a silent dinner with a very interesting conversation going on via notes. After he'd given our or-ders to the server and we had our wine and appetizers he had reached for the notepad and wrote something, sliding it over to me to read.

"Take off your jacket."

I still had the long, blue silk scarf draped over my shoul-ders and it hung loose just barely covering my breasts. I draped the jacket over the back of my chair. The scarf moved away from one breast and as I turned back towards our table, I noticed a woman sitting at a table across the way. She had, obviously, caught an eyeful of the demi bra nipple show through the strained white cotton of my shirt before I adjusted the scarf again to cover me. She smiled and returned her gaze to the man she was sitting with, but continued to look over at our table.

A few minutes later, Benjamin wrote something else on the notepad and slid it over to me to read. *"Unbutton the top of your blouse so I can see your cleavage."*

I had my elbows up on the table and brought my hands together so it looked like I was just resting my fingers there and when I put my hand back down to the table cloth, the button was opened and a juicy curve of breast was clearly visible now.

We ate silently and he would take a slow deep breath occasionally and tent his fingers under his chin, leaning forward on the table. He would stop and run those slender fingers around the rim of his wine glass in lazy circles while he looked at me and then down at the mound of breast I had exposed.

The woman at the other table had caught my button magic and I saw her lean forward and her stare was now more direct. I gave a small smile, letting her know that I was aware of my audience.

He wrote on the notepad again and slipped it over to me.

"Go to the restroom and take off your g-string. Give it to me when you return."

I looked up from the note and maintained eye contact with him as I rose from my chair with my clutch bag. I trailed my hand over his shoulder as I passed him by, grazing his neck lightly with my red painted nails.

As I passed her table several yards ahead, I looked over towards the woman and our eyes met for a moment. I saw a look of heat and wonder in them before she turned back to the man at her table.

I had just come out of the stall where I'd removed my g-string and I was tucking it into my clutch when she entered the room. She stood next to me at the mirror as I reapplied my red lipstick and tamed a few stray hairs that had escaped their place.

"I couldn't help but notice the notes you two are passing and that you seem to be playing some sort of game," she said shyly. "Is it fun? We're in a bit of a rut right now in our sex life and watching you two is making me a bit jealous and excited. I hope you don't mind me asking."

"No, I don't mind." I opened my clutch and showed her the g-string. I told her the contents of the notes and about the lingerie gift at my door so she had the full picture of the dare- fantasy game that Benjamin was playing; seeing how far I would go when he challenged me.

"God! That is so hot. I have a notebook in my purse. If I take my panties off and write my husband a note telling him what I did, do you think he'd be excited?"

"Sweetheart, if you do that, you won't last until dessert before he drags you home to eat you alive. Just keep watching what I do and follow my lead. My lover always comes up with some very interesting things for me to do." She thanked me and as she headed into the stall to start her own game, I made my way back to our table.

I had my clutch open as I walked and pretended to be looking for something. As I arrived just behind Benjamin's chair, I took the g-string in my hand and slipped in under his jacket and into the breast pocket. I patted the pocket and kissed his ear before I took my seat again.

It was a small table and I felt him slide his feet between mine and move my legs slightly apart. By this time, the woman had returned to her table and seated herself across from her husband with a wicked smile on her face. She slipped her own note across the table towards him and looked back up at me. Her eyes grew wide as she glanced down and saw Benjamin's feet moving my legs, the little bit of my exposed pussy and the edge of the garter belt that was visible now.

We ate our entrée's and he poured more wine for us. He sat back in his chair and his eyes burned a hole in my cleavage as he drank. He took his pen and wrote something and very slowly slid it across to me.

"Touch your pussy and give me your hand."

This would be challenging. While I was pondering how, exactly, in this lovely restaurant, that I could manage to touch my own pussy without everyone seeing, I saw the woman watching intently to see what I had been told to do next. Her husband was leaning towards her now and held one of her hands across their table. He must have liked her note.

I moved my napkin on my lap and intentionally caught my scarf along with it. As the scarf fell down, giving Benjamin a nice view of the hard nipples dancing at the edge of the lace, I reached down to retrieve it and deftly slipped a right hand finger into my very wet pussy at the same time. I adjusted my scarf with my left hand to cover my breasts again and reached my hand across the table to him.

The woman was watching intently and caught my finger move. I was too far away to hear her breath catch, but it did. Benjamin took my hand and raising it to his mouth he kissed my fingers and snuck in a lick while wearing a wicked smile.

We passed on a dessert course, knowing that what waited back at the apartment would be sweeter than any chocolate treat they had at Vincent. Feeling very turned on and bold by now, I rose from my chair and Benjamin reached to help me put my jacket back on. Instead, I took it and tucked it over my arm and he walked half a step behind me with one hand on my back. I slid the scarf from my neck and held it trailing in my other hand and walked out with my hard nipples on display for anyone else who watched me go. There were glares from some female patrons and some nods of approval to Benjamin from men who watched me leaving the restaurant.

As I passed the table of the other woman, I trailed my left hand out. She reached for mine and we slid our palms across each others in a woman's high five as I made my way with Benjamin towards our cars.

"Did you know that woman?" he asked leaning into my convertible, his curiosity piqued.

"No... But she was watching us." I knew I'd just upped the ante on his game now by enlisting my eager voyeur friend. I gave a husky laugh and peeled out of the parking lot towards my apartment so he'd have to chase me back to collect the juicy present that I had waiting for him to unwrap.

I made it to my apartment before he did and I had just gotten the key in the door. He must have been running because he was right behind me and kicking the door shut again behind him. Since my panties were conveniently in his pocket, it took all but a moment to unzip his suit pants and get his cock free from his boxers.

Benjamin shoved me up against the wall in my front hallway and I hoisted one leg up around his hip so he could slide his cock into me. Pinned against the wall with my chest crushed against his and the fingers of his left hand wound tightly into my hair, he thrust into me over and over again.

"I'm just going to use you right now because I won't last to get you upstairs. I'll take care of you later, so hold on; this is going to be fast and hard."

I braced myself on the wall with one hand. "Just do it. I can't wait either."

With exquisite effort on his face, Benjamin thrust hard and deep and fast inside me until he shuttered with an orgasm and slumped against me there in the hall.

"So, this foreplay thing really does work, eh?"I said, and we laughed as we clung to each other catching our breath and I was already getting excited for what else he had planned for upstairs.

*"Sex is not the answer. Sex is the question.
'Yes' is the answer."*

Swami X

Chapter 3

San Diego 1972

Beginner's Luck

If Eros is watching over you the first time you have sex, it will be with somebody that takes your breath away. I've heard some awful first-time sex stories, and some funny ones as well, and some that are just about perfect. Mine was lucky and nearly perfect in a teenage sort of way.

Aidan had a lean, long body with lightly muscled arms and a rear end that was made for jeans and touching. He wore the casual perfection of youth like a crown; easily and worthy of it. His brown hair fell in waves around his face so he looked like he'd just come inside off a windy beach. He had a crooked smirk of a smile and an over the top, cocky swagger that made the girls at school do a hair flip, head tilt, eyelash batting sigh when he passed them in the halls on his way to class.

I never was a hair flipping sort of girl, but I knew what I liked and for me, direct eye contact always got my motor running. Apparently it got his running to and we found ourselves, many times, backed against a wall somewhere private, with him leaning into me and my hands jammed in the back pockets of his jeans while we swapped spit and went a little further all the time.

Maybe it's that first bad boy experience and the invisible hook he sunk into my panties the first time he kissed my mouth, but this boy had me signed, sealed and delivered before the first time he moved his lips off mine. All it took was that searing eye contact across a room and a nod towards a rendezvous spot and I would follow behind him like a girl possessed to whatever corner, shady place or vacant room where he wanted to bring me.

He was like a scratchy surface and I was a match and every time we rubbed together, we risked burning a building down. We came very close to closing the deal one New Year's Eve until someone interrupted us and it would be months before he would be home from his out of state college again for another try.

It was June and hot and people were gathered at the home of a friend and the party was loud and crowded. Making my way through the wall to wall bodies, and stopping to talk with friends, I located the beer and filled the plastic cup I'd been offered. The crowd had me stuck now in the kitchen and I could hear yells and cheering when the front door opened and Aidan wandered in.

Just hearing his name caused a flame to rip through my belly so I maneuvered my way to a place where I could watch unseen as the crowd noise followed him in, reaffirming his local hero status.

He was looking mighty fine in a Stones Sticky Fingers tour shirt, jeans and western boots. From where I was watching I could see him work the room collecting a dozen shoulder bumps and back slaps from the guys and hopeful hugs from twittering girls as he blazed a path across the party. Our host threw an arm around his shoulder and leaned in so he could hear Aidan's question and then tilted his beer bottle towards the wall where I was standing.

Aidan turned to scan the crowd and when our eyes met, that crooked smirk spread across his face and suddenly, for me, there was no one else was in the room. Knowing his M.O., it would be awhile before we spoke. He wasn't the kind to rush over to say hello and we didn't do public displays of affection, so we pretended it was no big deal that we happened to be at the same party.

You always think you're being very stealthy when you've located your target and you're trying to get laid, but the truth is, you may as well hang a neon sign around your neck and turn on a tornado siren. People know. Everybody knows. They always know.

The crowd filled back in and the music was cranked up even louder and I found myself just across the room talking with a few friends. He carried on his own conversations while leaning on a door frame and looking in my direction every few minutes as we kept tabs on our locations like a silent version of submarine radar pings. This time, when my gaze strayed casually towards him, he was looking straight at me. He gave me the familiar nod that meant I should follow him.

The old round the bases game we had been playing always left me feeling hungry for a meal I couldn't have and we were both miles past ready to light this bonfire we'd been throwing sticks and gasoline onto for the past two years. I followed to an empty bedroom at the house.

I stepped into the room a few seconds after him and he caught my arm and pulled my face towards his, tangling his fingers into my hair. His mouth was smoke and wine and hot and wet as those crazy soft lips moved on mine until I couldn't catch my breath. The heat from his body warmed up the Old Spice he wore and I inhaled deeply imprinting the taste and smell of him onto my senses.

He moved me over towards the bed, sliding his hands up under my cotton shirt, over my bra and around my back. He lifted my shirt up and I obliged by raising my arms for him. Aidan pressed his hands on my back and brought his mouth to mine again. The alcohol I had drunk had my brain soft and pliable and I relaxed into his movements.

His tongue worked its way to my throat and he nibbled and sucked that sensitive place just behind my earlobe. He ran his tongue up and down the cord in my neck and switched to the other side before I tipped over.

He reached then into the cups of my bra and lifted my breasts out until they were shelved on the under wires. "Wow. You are gorgeous," he murmured as his head sunk down and he took my right nipple into his hot mouth. I'd never felt this sensation before and it sent a jolt through my body. He moved to the other nipple, running his tongue around and around and sucking hard until I gasped. Free of my cotton bra, he ran his hands all over my breasts, lifting to feel the weight of each in his palm.

His hands moved to my jeans and in seconds, he had them unbuttoned and sliding down my thighs until they pooled at my ankles and I kicked them off somewhere into the room. He moved me sideways and with his tongue at my ear, he turned his hand so it was flat against my firm teenage belly and he slowly slid his fingers into my panties until they found soft hair. They kept going until they moved the lips of my cunt apart and he found the warm wetness he was seeking. He kept his hand there, stroking and twirling and raising moans from me.

My heart was pounding as I knew we'd finally arrived at home plate. When he stopped and pulled his own shirt over his head and stepped free of his pants, I gave an involuntary intake of breath on seeing him erect and pointing directly at what he wanted next.

He pulled me down on the bed and reached down to my pussy to gather some of my wetness that he smoothed over his shaft before he slid on the condom. I opened my legs for him as he climbed up between them and like soft thunder, he slid into me. Home run. He fit so well, like his cock was custom made for my pussy.

For half an hour we moved together as he pushed and glided, in and out, fast and slow, hard and soft, waiting and continuing, until I was like putty in his hands. Maybe it was the perfect placement of our pubic bones or the alignment of the stars but for my very first time, I rode his thrusts like an old hand at this and when we came, it was together and explosive.

We laughed out loud and he fell down across me exhausted. Sweat stuck our bodies together and when we finally peeled apart and he shook his wet hair back out of his eyes, they were shining.

"It's about fucking time you two!" We heard our host yell from the hallway as he banged on the door. We heard clapping and shouts from our friends cheering us on from outside. Gripped with wicked laughter, we grabbed our clothes and quickly pulled them on. I started back towards the party and he grabbed my hand, pulling me into his arms again and sealed the big night with a last moist kiss saying, "We should have done that, years ago."

Mine was a very lucky introduction to the wonderful world of sex. It was a perfect kind of beginner's luck.

"A gentleman is a patient wolf."

Henrietta Tiarks

Chapter 4

Tokyo, Japan 1987

Sakura: The Living Canvas

After some of my private session photography gained attention in the fine art world, I was invited to select a topic and create a collectors book with a well known publisher. There were several subjects I had always wanted to cover, but it seemed like the right time to pursue the art of Horimono: full body singular subject, art tattooing. I wrote my proposal for the publisher and they loved the idea and sent me a very substantial advance to get moving on its production.

This full body tattooing covers ankles all the way over the shoulders and down the arms to the wrists. The style developed in the late 1700's, after the Japanese government began the practice of tattooing criminals, often on the forehead, but always visible, with symbols describing their crime for anyone they encountered. It was a type of public humiliation and a deterrent for repeat offenders. The underground criminal world of Japan, the Yakuza, had their own artists create elaborate pieces of full body art to hide the signs of their criminal activities. Soon after, the art of Horimono was born. The traditional form of Horimono leaves any exposed skin beyond the shirt collar, wrist or bottom of pants unmarked, so the extent of the tattooing was a secret known only to the other Yakuza family members.

The painful and lengthy process, sometimes taking years and tens of thousands of dollars to complete, was a symbol of belonging and it was earned by members through their loyalty. The artist worked for two hours per day every third day on these lengthy projects as they would tire and the recipient was spared lengthier sessions of pain.

I got busy researching the best artists in the USA, Japan, Thailand, Singapore and Taiwan where an international conference and competition takes place yearly. I packed my gear and my always ready travel bags and headed out to gather images and stories for the book.

I decided to start at the Taiwan Conference where I could have a firsthand look at hundreds of styles of tattoo work all in one place. The atmosphere was carnival like and the artists and fans ran the gamut from senior citizens to teens. Most of what I saw was the random tattooing of unrelated symbols, sayings and kitschy designs, more like the basement bedroom walls of an angry 14 year old bi-polar boy. There were some specific tattoos that were small masterpieces in their detail and style, but they lost big points when fighting for the eyes attention with a pin-up girl or a saying in Sanskrit that may have translated to either "inner serenity" or "Americans are stupid". Unless you're a linguistics expert, it's likely the latter.

I headed back to the Horimono artists area and found a world apart from the rest of the carnival atmosphere of the conference. Here there were sweeping dragons whose feet began on the ankles and the detailed minutiae of scales and depth and luscious jewel tones swept up legs, across backs and settled their perfect faces over the shoulder where their realistic eyes could watch over their owner, keeping them safe from harm. Some were scenes from ancient paintings that told a tale as you started at the beginning and followed them around to their end. The bodies looked like kimono tapestries and I was intrigued with the idea that a person would volunteer to become a living canvas with one story for their entire lifetime.

It was easy for me to find men with the art form who allowed me to photograph them for the book. It was much harder to find women with true Horimono work who would do the same. After hearing my questions and knowing the respectful professionalism of my intent with this project, an older tattoo artist pulled me aside and slipped me a name and address in Japan, where I could meet a Geisha Girl with the kind of Horimono work I hoped to photograph.

There's a big difference between the traditional Geisha, a highly trained and skilled entertainer for polite companionship, and the Geisha Girl, a prostitute that wears a similar costume but performs sexual favors for her clients. If you're looking closely, you'll notice that the Geisha wears her obi sash tied in the back holding her kimono closed. The Geisha Girl wears hers tied in the front as she may have the need to open and close her kimono several times a day.

The Soapland Kabukicho district houses more than 300 sex shops and "hotels" and it was there that I met with the sex worker who had taken the name Sakura. Sakura means cherry blossom in Japanese and as the national tree, it appears in many forms on everything from greeting cards and art work to fabric and tattoos. Luckily for me, her English was fluent, so we were able to carry on an interview in the privacy of her rooms without an interpreter present. I was glad for that because I wanted photos of her Horimono, but I also wanted her story.

She told me that her father had owed a large debt to a local gang and when he was unable to pay, he arranged for his daughter to join the women of their brothels so she could work off his debt. As a sign of possession, she was made to undergo the multi year process of receiving the Horimono over her body. She said she was 27 years old and it had taken ten years to apply the full Horimono. They had begun the process when she was just 15.

She rose and showed me how she presented her body to her clients for their pleasure and she let me photograph as she did. Traditional Japanese music was playing and in this shoji screened space; the petite Asian beauty slowly loosened her kimono and artfully draped it back over her shoulders. I saw the branches then, gracefully winding their way across her upper back with pink and white cherry blossoms that seemed to be floating in the air. As she let the kimono fall, I saw that the tree began at her ankle and grew from there, up her slender legs with clusters of leaves and blossoms placed on her buttocks and creeping towards the crease of the cheeks. She reached behind her and spread the cheeks apart and I could see that small branches continued into that tender spot and a single bloom framed her anus using the opening in her body as the flower's center.

She turned then and I saw that the front of her body was covered with more branches and blossoms that curved around her breasts and again, the blooms had been inked with the multi needle tool right onto her nipples making them each a flower of their own. She stretched out her arm to show the affect of the branches that made their way down her arms to her delicate wrists. It was stunning to see though the physical pain that she endured to receive this art must have left her with some repercussions the world will never see.

I photographed her for the book and gathered as much information as I could in the two hours I had paid her for. When our time was ending, she asked me if I would like to stay and see her work from a viewing area that men often use when they pay to watch others. She led me around a corner and showed me where I could sit in the small private viewing booth that had a two way mirror installed for exactly this reason.

In a few minutes, the door to Sakura's room opened and a man entered wearing a business suit. He had left his shoes at the main door as was the custom so he stood in his stocking feet. He spoke to her for a moment and turned back towards the door and ushered in a second man, also in business attire. She bowed to them and they bowed back and she showed them to a place to sit and brought them drinks that looked to be scotch on the rocks, a very popular choice in Japan. Her music was playing and the soft lighting muted with paper shades over the lamps took some of the clinical aspect out of for hire sex.

She began her slow strip tease for them, as she had for me, baring shoulders and slowly sliding her kimono back off her shoulders as she began to reveal her art. They nodded in appreciation as they sipped their drinks. As she dropped the robe to the floor in a graceful puddle at her feet, she took a small step with one foot deftly parting her legs and with her hands she spread the cheeks of her small and firm ass revealing the flowered bud of her anus for the men. One said something and she nodded permission and he step forward to look more closely at the secret flower and to run his hands over her petals and the rounds of her ass.

She stood and turned, showing the men the elaborate art that covered her breasts and stomach and continued down the flesh of her thighs. In a move like a prima ballerina, she turned on one foot and raised the other straight up, grabbing her raised ankle and showing the men a full view of her vagina, shaved and also covered with vines and blossoms. She turned again and standing with her feet apart, she stretched both arms to her sides and invited the men to climb the tree.

They removed their clothing and folded it neatly setting it back on the chairs and one stepped in front of her and the other behind her. They began to run their hands over her body squeezing the nipple blossoms and grasping the firm rounds of her bottom.

They moved around her now and pulled nipples into their mouths as they suckled together on the blossoms. She swayed ever so slightly like a tree in the wind while they wound their hands and tongues where ever they wanted.

They said something to her and she stepped to a fabric curtain and brought a wedge shaped bolster that was flat at the top. She sat on the top of it and leaned back resting her shoulders on the incline. She raised her legs and opening them in a wide V. The men stepped to her, again, one on either side and each holding a thigh, they brought their mouths down and began to lick at each blossom their

31

tongues could touch. She held her legs like that for a long time, occasionally bending her knees down as their licking sent spasms through her small body. They plunged fingers into her pussy and her anus while they licked around their own hands until she orgasmed. She rose gracefully from the fallen tree pose.

Their cocks were hard and she said something and the men nodded and followed her to a low narrow padded bench that was sitting near the wall.

She had asked them to bring the bench to the center of the room and when they did, she asked one of the men to sit on the end of the bench and to lie back. She instructed the other man to stand behind her and she placed his hands on her hips. Leaning over the man lying on the bench she gently placed her hands on his hips and bent forward to take his cock into her mouth and she began to suck.

The standing man entered her pussy from behind and the three began to rock together causing the man fucking her to move her mouth down on the other man's cock. Before they had a chance to climax, the man on the bench spoke and I guessed he wanted to be inside her as well.

The standing man withdrew from her while the other stood to join them. She stood on tip toes and the larger of the two men lifted her up between them and she gripped her arms around his neck and wrapped her legs around his body. She lowered herself onto his cock. The second man dipped his fingers into the small jar of negiri that Sakura kept near the bench and he lubricated his cock with the white powdery looking substance that is made from mallow root, dry sea algae and oil. When he had coated his cock with the substance he pushed into her anus while he reached around her and grabbed her breasts for grip. Together they fucked her that way, one man moving in a steady rhythm while the cock in her ass was pumping fast. The men climbed the tree that way until they came.

They sat down on the bench then and drank the rest of their scotch, sated from their blossom meal.

She went to retrieve two bowls and towels and she proceeded to wipe down their sticky hands, mouths and cocks. She pulled her kimono back on while they dressed and when they were ready to leave, the man who had come into the room first bowed presenting her an envelope, her pay, in his two outstretched hands that were brought together like a prayer gesture with the envelope resting under his thumbs.

Watching this coupling and fantasy from behind the mirror in the small viewing room was an experience I will never forget. The presence of her Horimono covered body lent a surreal air to the raw sex happening in the shoji screened room.

I asked her later if she had pleasure doing this work and she said that there was a satisfaction in submitting to her client's fantasies. She said that her Horimono put her in a category as a specialty girl, almost superhuman, like a goddess. The clients who come to her desire to both possess and also to worship this goddess they imagine in this very intimate way.

The Japanese call this the Floating World; the fleeting and ephemeral world of pleasure. Surely, all of our places where sex happens are not that different from this floating world where stillness and peace are broken occasionally by heat and passion as we bring our bodies to full pleasure in whatever way the moment has called for.

"It is not the sex that gives pleasure, but the lover."

Marge Piercy

Chapter 5

San Diego 1979

Keira

I was living with Jackson now and Keira, our friend, lived on the East Coast but was often a guest in our house for extended stays so we had a lot of time to cook meals together, hike and take photographs. The three of us got along terrifically and Jackson and I always enjoyed her visits. She brought her great sense of humor, her willingness to help out and be a welcome house guest and her uncanny ability to fix things. She even taught me how to remove a carburetor from a motorcycle, clean it and reinstall it and how to ride, which led me to purchasing my first bike.

One evening, we got onto the subject of sex. We had finished a bottle of wine with the Italian dinner I'd made and I asked her when she first knew that she was a lesbian. As a teenager, a beautiful married woman had brought her to her bed when her husband was out. Their secret affair lasted for years. Keira had never really wanted to have sex with men, not ever. In earning her art degree, she'd had hours of life drawing and saw her share of men's bodies lounging casually as the class sketched them in various poses and growing up with brothers, had certainly seen them in the buff. It had just never interested her she said, until she started to wonder lately if perhaps she had been working off her fear of her stepfather. Maybe, just maybe, if she found the right situation, she might give men a try. I asked if she would feel safer if another woman was there too and she said maybe. We talked further and then, with a nod from Jackson we offered to bring her to our bed.

I took her hand and walked her towards our bathroom where the large walk in shower was. I took off Jackson's clothing and turned on the shower and he stepped in under the water. I took off my own clothing and joined him there and we started to soap our bodies and slowly rub each other and we opened our arms for her to join us. She stepped in fully clothed and laughed nervously. After only a few moments, she said she just couldn't do it. We told her that was perfectly fine and if she ever changed her mind, all she had to do was ask and we would bring her into this circle of trust.

It wasn't until a year later on her next visit that something did happen, but it wasn't with the three of us and Jackson didn't know because the fire we started between us was hot and I wanted the heat for myself. Jackson was out of town for a few days. It had been raining like mad and we were soaked to the bone by the time Keira and I got back to the house from shopping in town. Laughing like crazy as we ran in the door, I headed to the back of the house for towels and I yelled for her to grab the white wine in the refrigerator and some snack things for a floor picnic.

Returning to the living room, I tossed a towel over her head and she rubbed her short blond hair vigorously until it stood up in spikes. I laughed hard when she revealed her hairstyle and she grabbed the second towel and tossing it over my head, rubbed my long root beer colored hair until it was a tangled mess hanging down in my eyes. "Let's see how great your hair looks after this!"

I was still laughing as I pushed the mess back off my forehead, she saw that I had a strand of hair hanging down in my face and reached out and moved it back behind my ear. "Pan, you really are a very beautiful woman. You know that, right?" I must have looked puzzled and said I may be "interesting" looking but not beautiful, but she insisted I was wrong.

"Oh come on Keir, you've known me, how many years, and you just decided this now?" She said she had decided that the day we met but she knew I was into men so she admired me from afar. "Come on. You have to know that dark Franco-Mediterranean look of yours is very exotic for a Scandinavian like me; it's like catnip. Those luscious breasts and your perfect rear end; you're the lesbian wet dream."

I was surprised and flattered and some small match lit a fire between my legs and made me bold. I turned to her and said, "Show me. Show me who you are as a lover."

She took my chin in her hands to tilt my face up and pressed her lips to mine. It was soft as a whisper. No stubble, no roughness like a man's lips; just softness and heat. I was amazed at how easy it was for me to reach to her and loosen the buttons of her wet flannel shirt and peel it off revealing her cotton tank top and her lovely, small and firm breasts. I lifted the wet shirt over her head and reached out a hand to touch the soft orb. Keira smiled as she watched this first timer discover a new world. I ran my knuckles over her cool skin, still damp from the rain soaked clothing, and goose bumps covered her flesh as I trailed my hand down and onto her flat, firm stomach.

She reached to me and helped me out of my t-shirt that was still clinging to me. The rain and the heat of the moment had contracted my nipples to two hard points beneath it. My lacy bra was next to go after she took a moment to run her finger along the edges of the lace. "The first time I really saw these breasts was that day in the shower with Jackson. I think about them a lot." I watched her like it was a dream as she caught my nipple between her fingers and gently pinched it before she brought her soft mouth down onto it to suck. The jolt that hit my pussy when she ran her tongue around the tip and then sucked the whole nipple into her mouth made me toss my head back with pleasure.

Keira took my hand and led me back to the guest room where she stayed when visiting us. I had been traveling in Europe and Morocco a few years earlier and I'd decorated this room in jewel tones of purple and teal and deep burgundy with tapestries and gold threaded fabrics and candles anywhere I could tuck them. It was made for sex. I lit the candles and stood in the center of the room to remove my pants, now wet with more than rain. She slid out of her pants and we stood with our nakedness pressing together, while she held me in her arms and kissed me deeply, artfully swirling her tongue as she sucked mine and kissed my mouth. She moved to my neck and did something that I have since taught other lovers. Tilting my head to one side, she stiffened her tongue and ran it from just below my ear down the tense cord of my neck, up and down, up and down with the wetness of her saliva. I was moaning by the time she guided me back and to the bed. The light coming through the matchstick bamboo shade was turning pink in the setting sun.

Before I fell back onto the softness of the bedcovers, she reached behind me and firmly held my ass in her hands. She ran her hands down the back of my legs and squatted down to bring them up the front of my thighs slow and sensually and as her hand reached my pussy, she dipped a finger in and feeling the wetness there, she said, "You're ready now." As she made her way up my body she licked from my abdomen to my breast and stopping to give a caress to one and a wet suck to the other. Keira guided me back onto the bed and with my legs over the edge; she knelt down between them and pushed them open with her shoulders.

I gathered some pillows from above my head and propped myself up so I could watch as a woman took my body for the first time. She gave me a wicked smile and brought her hot mouth to my slit teasing out the throbbing button hidden in the folds of pink. She licked expertly and sucked at my clit and my body experienced wave upon wave of pleasure at the deed she was doing and the thrill that it was a she doing this to me. Her slender fingers found their way into me and while her tongue played at this tender place and she began to work her hand in and out of me in a rhythm that had me writhing to its beat. A crashing orgasm hit, making me arch my back off the mattress.

I barely caught my breath when the need to taste her the same way took me over. I pulled her up onto the bed and covered her breasts with wandering hands and tongue and snaked my way down between her legs to the downy

39

blond patch that hid my meal. I pushed her legs up so her knees were bent and wriggled my way between them until I could touch my first pussy that wasn't mine. I gently parted the labia. I had seen my own vagina in a mirror, but this was a wet dream come true, to see and touch and taste what lovers had seen and touched and tasted of me before. "It's like the petals of a wild rose," I said.

"Well, Georgia wasn't wrong." The O'Keefe reference made me laugh and I remembered our road trip to the museum in Santa Fe and all those glorious open flowers she had painted. Keira had caught me admiring a particularly lovely Grey Line piece with multi colored elongated layers leading to a dark unknown center. She had come up behind me and whispered in my ear "Vagina." It shifted the way I saw the rest of the exhibit and I now had another reason to be intrigued by that painter.

I gently parted her petals and with great care slid a finger into the moist cave, feeling the ridges inside and the outer petals now slick with Keira's juices. It was time to taste the flower. As I moved closer, I could feel the hair tickle my lips and I moved my tongue in a long lick from the bottom of the petals and up to the clit. I looked up between her legs to see if she was watching me and when she smiled, I put my face back down to bury it in this juicy place and feast on her. I flattened my tongue for long licks and added small sucks, like sipping a straw, directly on her clit while my fingers moved inside her sopping wet pussy until she climaxed hard and laughed saying "Are you sure you haven't done this before?"

"You taste like toasted almonds." I said with her cum juices on my lips. She said that when you don't eat meat and your diet was mostly fruits and vegetables, that you had a more delicate flavor. I climbed back up on the bed and kissed her mouth with her own juices covering my lips. I hadn't thought of Jackson once the whole time we women were exploring each other. Pulling the indigo shawl from the side table, I flung it across our bodies and we fell asleep, tangled like cats with her hand cupping my breast and my leg thrown over her muscled ass.

For days we were stealing secret kisses with other people in the next room, sliding her hand down my pants in a stolen moment and fucking each other like cats in heat when we finally found ourselves alone again. I didn't tell Jackson until several months later. He said it was good I was still exploring because he had been seeing someone as well. He and I ended soon after that. Keira and I still keep in touch, though we never were lovers again.

"A chicken and an egg are lying in bed. The chicken is smoking a cigarette with a satisfied smile on its face and the egg is frowning. The egg mutters to no one in particular, "I guess we answered that question."

Author Unknown

Chapter 6

Los Angeles 1978

Too Much Of a Good Thing

My car had broken down on a local road and after cursing a blue streak, I got out to reluctantly start my walk to the gas station a mile back. While I grabbed my sunglasses from their perch in my hair and adjusted the bag on my shoulder, a car slowed down and the passenger window slid open. Always ready for whackos, I was prepared to launch into a verbal assault that would leave a sane man running for cover when I heard him call out. "Pan? Is that you?"

I lifted my glasses and hunched down to look into the sports car window and there sat a guy I hadn't seen in years. We had gone to school together and though he was a few years ahead of me, he was a hot fantasy of every female at school.

"Royal Stanton, well I'll be damned."

"Looks like you've got some car trouble."

"Yep. This vehicle has crapped out on me for the last time."

"Come on. Hop in. I'll give you a ride."

I took him up on the offer and while we rode towards the station to arrange for a tow, he asked what I was up to that night. I had nothing on my calendar so we decided to grab some food and catch up on news.

Over burgers and beers we laughed and talked about people we knew, coaches and team standings, family businesses and what we were doing now; his budding architecture firm and my photography that sometimes paid the bills and sometimes not. The conversation flowed and we were having such a good time that he suggested I come back to his place and we could continue our visit.

I'd almost forgotten how strikingly handsome he was with fine, strong bone lines and brown eyes that were the color of rich, dark coffee.

His place was large and contemporary with art that didn't come from a catalog or a paint by number set. He had leather sofas, a kitchen filled with expensive appliances and stocked like a real adult would have stocked it; a very nice change from the man boys who were still reliving their adolescence with brick and board shelves that held no books, only two ugly candles and a bong.

He put a fire in the hearth and opened a nice bottle of wine that he poured into glasses that were so thin they rang like a clear bell when my fingernail tapped the side. I settled into a sofa and he fit himself in next to me as we continued our little reunion. After a while, he excused himself and when he came back, he looked alert and frisky. He eased down next to me and pulled me towards him saying, "You are definitely not 15 anymore and it's a good thing because after what I'd like to do with you, I'd be in prison."

He brought his mouth to mine and he wound his strong arms around me pulling us close together. He was very tall and though I'm taller than the average woman, he towered over me at well over 6'4". I felt like a fairy princess wrapped in all that manliness and he easily scooped me up and moved me to the soft rug in front of the fire.

He sat down and pulled me up onto his lap, straddling him and finished the kiss he had started a few moments earlier. I lifted off his shirt and ran my hands over the powerful shoulders he kept toned in his home gym. I reached to take off his glasses and set them on the coffee table. "All right Clark Kent, let's have a look at Superman, in the flesh." My voice was husky and purring and he tilted his head back to laugh leaving me a gorgeous throat to blaze kisses across.

He unbuttoned every one of the small pearl buttons on my cashmere cardigan and when he saw the French black lace bra I wore beneath it, he sighed, "Delicious." He unclasped the front of the bra and eased my breasts out before discarding it on the floor behind us. Bare soft breasts mashed up against his hard chest as he ravaged my neck with tongue and teeth, nibbling and licking his way from ear to ear.

I was turned on by his warm skin touching me and with a smooth motion he rose to his knees, tipping me backwards and removed my pants. He left the panties on and he slid his hands up and down the insides of my legs like a rowing motion. He'd done this same motion countless times on the crew team at school. After this night, I'd never watch a boat race the same way again. Each stroke brought his fingertips closer and closer to the edge of my panties until he touched me just under the fabric and teased the tender flesh of my pussy. He grabbed a pillow from the sofa and raising my hips, he slid it under my ass so I was open and propped on this make shift shelf just the right height for him when his elbows held him up and his mouth slid up where his hands had been.

"Oh, you have definitely done this before." I teased. He just smiled before his face moved down to the hot snatch I offered up to him like an appetizer. With his finger of his right hand, he slid the fabric to the side and a second later I felt his wet, hot tongue lapping at my clit. He ran his tongue front to back and around the post like a barrel racing horse doing figure eights. He deposited some of his saliva and darted his tongue inside me occasionally just to hear my breath catch. When the panties were as wet as my pussy, he slid them off. And on returning to his work, he used his left hand to separate the folds of my pussy. He plunged the fingers of his right hand deep into me causing my back to arch from the sensation and when his fingers were good and wet, he slid one down and pressed it into the other hole while keeping a rhythm of in and out, pussy and ass, while his tongue licked and his lips sucked me to a mind shattering orgasm.

I was still breathing hard when I realized he still had his pants on. "No fair. Lose the pants mister. It's my turn to mess you up." He laughed and got to his feet to loosen the belt and drop his pants and boxers high above me. When his cock was visible, my eyes must have flown wide because he laughed again at my reaction to the largest, thickest penis I have ever seen. "Wow. No wonder why they named you Royal."

I was up on my knees in an instant and directing him to lie back on the same rug he had ravaged me on. Once he was settled, I slithered up on him until my mouth was perched above his throbbing cock. I lowered my lips over him, taking as much of him as I could. He sighed and with my hand, I gathered some of my own juices and proceeded to slide my slippery hand up and down the shaft while I tongued and sucked the head and upper shaft. It was the best I could do to handle every inch of him at the same time. He remained so hard I couldn't believe it and after a few almost explosions he cried mercy and made me stop.

I crawled up towards his face and his hands found my waist while he lifted me higher so my full and dangling breasts could fit easily into his waiting mouth. Every suck brought a pull on my clit from inside and he grabbed my hips and positioned my pussy over his mouth. He tongued and licked and had me bucking like a bronco again.

He stopped abruptly to guide my hungry cunt onto his hungrier cock. I slid down onto him gasping at the girth that filled me side to side. I tried to work a few inches in at a time until I finally had the whole thing buried all the way. I had to stop a second and then I started to move, slowly at first, raising myself all the way up until he was almost out of me and then all the way down again like a carousel ride. He still hadn't come yet and I was wondering if it would ever happen.

"Is this good for you?" I asked. "Oh, hell yeah. Don't stop, Pan." So I followed his direction and continued my private pole dance. After a few more minutes, when he knew my cunt was accustomed to his gigantic cock, he lifted me off him and came around to slide into me from behind.

My face went down on the carpet and my ass rode high in the air as he plunged and pulled out again working me like rodeo horse. After what felt like forever, he finally gave a few more ramming thrusts and came with a loud moan. He held me still another minute letting his cock feel the final small pulses while inside me. My pussy felt spent and we lay there catching our breath for while.

When we had recovered, he pulled a throw blanket from the back of a chair and circled my shoulders with it. Getting up to fetch another bottle of wine from his cellar, I watched him walk away and seeing his now soft cock hanging like a thick rope moving against his thigh as he went, I was stunned, again, that he'd had that monster hidden in his pants every day of our childhood and I never knew.

As my mind was doing it's little time travel trip, he had made his way back to the living room and he grabbed our wine glasses. With his free hand extended he gave me a pull up. He handed me the bottle and keeping my hand firmly in one of his, he led the way up the stairs to his room.

It was stylish and he kept it neat. Not obsessively so, but you could tell he had an architect's eye in where he placed furniture and lighting. There was a small step at the foot of his bed that didn't make much sense when I first saw it and the king size bed was covered in navy satin sheets as blue as the deep ocean.

He poured more wine and I drank while I browsed his music collection. He fussed with his sound system and adjusted the temperature in the room a bit higher than it had been. Soon we were surrounded with jazz and warmth and he removed a small bottle from his tableside.

When he was ready, he took my hand and led me to the small step where he instructed me to put both my feet, facing the bed. He gently pushed me over into a bending position with my straight arms holding me up off the bed and then he slid the blanket slowly off me like a sculptor revealing a statue.

"Stay right here," he said, and made his way over towards the head of the bed where a floor length mirror I hadn't noticed had been facing towards his closet. He dragged the mirror to the side of the bed and turned it until I could see myself from the side as I turned my head slightly.

Returning to my on display ass, he took the bottle he had retrieved and pouring some of the slippery lubricant into his hands he rubbed them together, warming the liquid slightly. "Move your feet apart." I obliged and found that he had put some sort of gripping surface on the step so your feet wouldn't come off. He'd given a lot of thought to his sex games and he even had props, a first for me.

With his slippery hand, he coated my pussy and the cheeks of my ass, sliding his hands over me like he was waxing a Ferrari. Adding more oil, he brought his hands around and slicked up my dangling breasts and he used his fingers to pinch and twist my nipples until I let out a small cry of pleasure/pain. He went back behind me again and walking right up to my waiting cunt, he could slide into me when I was up on this lift. Now the step was making sense. As tall as he was, women just needed this little bit of altitude for him to be able to stand and penetrate them from behind. He stood, legs locked and grabbed my hips to pull me back onto him and told me to watch my breasts swing in the mirror while he took me from behind.

What a view this was, to see his shaft moving in and out and my tits swinging like a stripper at a men's club.

It was so oddly hot that I couldn't take my eyes off the mirror. He ran his hands over my slippery ass and reached one hand around the front of me to finger my clit. The thumb of his other hand slid into my ass, fingers splayed on my cheek for grip. By now, I was so hot and into it that he was standing still and I was responding to stimulation by pushing with my arms, driving me back onto his monstrous cock.

"Stand up now," he instructed. This pinched my ass cheeks together and gripped his cock harder and he moaned. "Now feel your breasts and watch as you do it."

I did. My hands slid through the oil like I was showering and over the mounds of my breasts. I grabbed both and squeezed and used the fingers of both my hands to pinch and roll my nipples while he slid in and out of me from behind with his face turned towards the mirror so he wouldn't miss a second of our sex show. "You're so damn hot. I could watch you all night."

His obvious pleasure made me feel hotter and I began to move my body in undulations like a pole dancer giving him a private show and his gratitude was obvious as the sweat poured down his brow and across his muscled chest while he worked. He came hard again and we collapsed on the bed.

My pussy was starting to ache and as the night wore on, we went several more rounds. I had noticed by the third one, that it wasn't me he was looking at in his carefully placed mirror, it was him. He was watching his arms flex and his face as he strained and I started to wonder if I might be interrupting his date with himself. After our flow of conversation earlier in the evening, the only thing he had to say now was a sex instruction or a request for something that enhanced his pleasure. He managed to maneuver me into all sorts of positions without making eye contact after the first round. Somewhere around three A.M., he had me on all fours on the bed and watching himself as he took me again, from behind.

I was beginning to feel a bit like an interchangeable prop for his sex games, but being young and stupid, I wanted to see where this was going.

By the sixth round, I had concluded that this guy was a robotic fucking machine. He was so into his own little world that I could have slipped out of the room and replaced myself with a blow up doll or a sheep and he might not have even noticed I was gone until he heard the bleating sound of his new partner. Certain now that his ego was even bigger than his cock but that he was otherwise harmless and seeing as I was too goddamn tired at that point to get up and call a taxi, when he mercifully fell asleep, so did I.

When I woke in the morning, I very quietly got up to take a shower in his large walk in. With my eyes covered with soap and shampoo running down my back to my ass crack, I didn't notice that he had joined me there under the running water until I felt the hardness of his cock knocking against my back and his large hands reaching around me, cupping my slippery breasts.

He turned me around in the tight circle of his arms and with his hands under my armpits; he lifted me up and onto him. My back and my ass cheeks were pressed against the cold ceramic tiles and he bounced me up and down on his cock again until I had to ask him to stop.

I love a good fuck and a tongue bath as much as the next girl, but I'd had enough and it was just time to stop.

Women are always saying how if they ever found a well hung man with the stamina to keep up with them, they could go all night, but believe it or not, there is a point when it becomes too much of a good thing.

My lips were sore from sucking and kissing. My pussy was aching. My clit was raw and my nipples were chafed from his teeth and tongue.

"Royal, how the hell were you able to keep going like that all night?" I asked.

"Cocaine. Want some?"

I declined and after pulling my clothes together and sharing some coffee, he gave me a ride back home. Just before I got out of his car, he pulled me to him and planted a wet kiss on my tender mouth. "I'll call you later. OK?"

"No. Don't. I think we're done. It was good to see you again and thanks for a very ... memorable night, but I think we're done."

He looked confused as he pulled away but he honored my request. I've never heard from him again and though I'll never forget that night, I don't have any desire to repeat it. Well, not with him at least. I hoped he'd be happy with whomever or whatever replaced me.

"Nymphomaniac: a woman as obsessed with sex as the average man."

Mignon McLaughlin

Chapter 7

Santa Monica 1980

Ollie & Pan Head Over Heels

I met Oliver in Los Angeles while doing some still publicity shots for a film. I spent several days on a set taking photographs of production and filming that their marketing department could use for press releases and teasers on Entertainment Weekend and in fan magazines.

Ollie was a personal trainer by day and a stunt double by night. Being roughly the same body type and same skin tone as a very well known action star, he was also on set waiting his turn to jump in and do the really difficult things that the former pro wrestler turned actor wasn't allowed to do for insurance reasons.

Over the next ten years, we found ourselves in the same city several times and whenever our schedules were free, we set a play date together. If there had been a constant man anywhere near my life, it would be Ollie. He had an easy laugh and told amazing stories complete with dramatic hand gestures that he learned from his South Pacific Islander/Italian family. I don't usually go for that muscled up kind of guy as most that I've met had far more developed meat in their abs than in their heads. Ollie, on the other hand was a bit of a geek trapped in an Adonis' body. He was smart and kind and he could make me laugh myself sick which he did, every time we met. And there was the sex. Ah yes, the sex.

One of the things he and I had in common was a healthy appetite for exploring the wonders of the human body that was almost as big as our need to be independent. Ollie was the perfect fuck buddy.

He loved that some of my photographic work was erotic and not only did I take the pictures for others but I could also feel the heat from the subjects as well.

We were game for whatever fantasy the other came up with, but one of our favorite play date activities was looking through erotic magazines together while Ollie would tell me what he would do with the model starting from that particular position. He would bring issues he'd collected and I would bring the ones that I had found in my travels. We would spread the photos out on the floor and work our way through several taking turns creating fantasy scenes out loud and soon enough, we would be acting out a few that we found the hottest.

As a surprise once, I had brought along some prints from a private photo session I'd done. It got Ollie even hotter than usual because I could add back story and a first person account of the gorgeous flesh I laid out for his eyes.

Ollie was strictly a pussy man so the photos I'd brought were only of women. He was especially intrigued with a blonde starlet I had photographed for her older, manager boyfriend.

Sheila was rather petite at 5' 4" and had a very full double d cup size. Her ass was round and heart shaped when she got on her hands and knees and the all over tan, I saw, was truly all over except for the small patch of pubic hair that was shaped like an elongated heart and bejeweled with pink crystals along her vagina lips. The hair was as platinum on her pussy as it was on her head; salon magic to be sure. I was guessing that most of the grooming and tanning was more for her man than for her.

The client chose not to be there for the photo session and he didn't trust any other men around his property, so he hired me if I would photograph alone with his girl. The day of the shoot, he handed me a box of props and a very detailed list of shots he wanted before he left me to my work. He may have had some mob connections but I never asked questions like that. He wanted his "girl" in an array of bondage outfits with a few very specific requests on his part. I'm sure she had no clue what he'd requested either, but he definitely had a bit of a master/slave thing going with this over eager twenty something beauty.

While she was lying on her back for some shots he had requested, I saw that her breasts were still firm and high, so unlike most women's that naturally fall to the sides when we lay down. I had to ask if her breasts were implants and she came over and put my hands on them so I could feel that they were all natural. Ollie made me give the tactile description of my little feel up moment with this juicy girl and said that one day he was going to bring me a surprise.

Ollie picked out a series of pictures where the woman was dressed in a red rubber bustier that tapered to a point at the top of her ass, thigh high fish net stockings and red high heels. For these photos he had wanted to see her squatting down onto a very large dildo and he insisted that she use it until she climaxed while I captured the scene.

It gave Ollie one of his "great ideas" and he stripped me down to my cami top and had me squat over him keeping my hands away so the only contact we had was his cock in my pussy. From that interesting position, I bounced up and down the way a jockey rides a race horse, floating above the saddle. Ollie closed his eyes and let me ride to the finish line. In that position, his cock went incredibly deep into me and I had more control over him than any other position. I would slide down, almost touching his lap and as I rose up, I clenched my cunt muscles with all my strength, squeezing his cock and milking him as I rose. His mind blowing orgasm was followed by a howl like a wolf on the hunt and raucous laughter at this new discovery. I highly recommend this position to anyone wanting to try something just a bit different with their partner. We called it the Squat and it became a favorite sex position for us and we made sure every time we had a play date, to work that little number in.

As he sifted through more of the photos, he asked me the story behind a certain standing pose. The instructions had been to have her standing facing the wall. Her wrists were tied together with velvet ropes and held up on a bar overhead and he wanted her ankles tied together and a blindfold over her eyes.

I asked Sheila if this was ok with her and she said it was all right to do, it was one of Lou's favorite things. When he took her from behind, he said her ass cheeks would grab his cock this way and make her pussy even tighter because he had to work his way into her. He had full control over her to do whatever he wanted, even spinning her in a different direction, and restrained like that made him really hot. Sometimes he would spank her ass while she was like that. He liked to see his red hand prints on her ass cheeks. He liked it when she was a little afraid of him and she said he always bought her something nice after he did it.

I asked her if she enjoyed it or was it something she did just for him. She told me that sometimes, when his hand would contact her pussy when he spanked her, she would cum, so yeah, she must like it.

Ollie listened and then asked if I was game to try any of this. I'm a control freak by nature and pretty strong for a woman so most of the sex partners I've had I could have done damage to easily if the game got out of control. This was Ollie though, a 6'5", 250 pound stunt man who was built like a rock. That alone sent a small ripple of fear through me and it also had me wondering how I would handle another moment of surrender in the hands of another human being. Shades of Benjamin shadowed through me from the year I spent doing just that, just for him.

We were at Ollie's place in Santa Monica and he had a fully equipped gym on the lower level. He used the gym for training sessions for his private clients, many of whom were action stars getting their bodies in shape to play a role where they had to look, for one film, like Ollie always does.

He gathered a few things from his room and led me down to the gym. My heart was beating pretty fast but I was still in. Over at the pull up bar he had me put my hands out in front and he tied my silk scarf around my wrists securely and brought my arms up over my head and tied them to the bar. I was wearing a push up bra and lace front thong panties and he unhooked the front of the bra so my breasts were exposed. He tied a bandana around my eyes and gave me a kiss saying he would take care of me. With my hands out of the way, he used his fingertips to trace delicate lines all the way down my body spreading goose bumps across my skin, sending shivers of pleasure and anticipation.

He had brought a few things with him but I hadn't expected the ice he put on my nipple, so cold it made me shake my head and cry out. He ran the ice over my other nipple and before I knew what was happening, he pressed the cube up into my pussy, turned me around and brought his hand down and spanked my ass. I barely caught my breath when he spanked me again, this time his big hand made some contact with my pussy and much to my surprise I let out an "oooo" and not an "oww". He delivered a few more solid smacks to my tender bottom. Between the icy cold of the cube in my cunt and the hot flash of his hand on my ass, I was overwhelmed.

He loosened the hand tie a bit and as soon as I started to bend forward to ease the strain in my shoulders, his strong hand connected again across both cheeks taking advantage of my bent over body. My pussy was buzzing as he followed with more electric smacks to my bottom. Each slap to my cunt sent a wave that started as pain and ended as pleasure and I found myself flinging my head back as my excitement mounted.

He loosed my hands and pulled me down over his lap and gently rubbed my stinging ass until I thought I was safe. Just as I started to relax, he connected again with a stinging spank asking me what I was feeling. Smack! He gave a few more loud spanks and a jolt of heat moved from the bottom of my feet, through my pussy.

When my ass was a bright rosy red he stopped and took off the blindfold and brought me to the mirror so I could see his handiwork. He liked what he saw and cradled my ass in his hands to sooth the stinging. I told him it was interesting, but ultimately, too degrading for me and I could take it off my list of favorite things.

He said that's too bad because he was getting into it and when I tried to give him a smack on his ass so he'd have a frame of reference for my discomfort, he just laughed and scooped me up. He must have had circuit training on his mind because I found myself clipped into inversion boots with my feet a foot apart and I was up ended in moments, watching him strip down from my upside down view. As he walked up to me, I saw that his cock was at my mouth and that my pussy was right there for his tasting.

He buried his tongue in me as I reached for his cock and pulled him to me for a tongue bath of my own. I didn't last long as I was laughing from the x-rated Cirque Du Soleil view of us in the gym mirrors and all the blood that was rushing to my head so he stopped and lifted me up and off the inversion rack.

We decided we probably weren't very good at this bondage thing. Maybe if the place was more dungeon-y type apparatus and less L.A. Rams training room, we would have played our roles better; but you have to work with what you have. We also agreed that he was going to have a hard time watching his clients on those two pieces of equipment without getting a hard on from here on out.

"How would you like to feel the way she looks?"

Groucho Marx

Chapter 8

Los Angeles 1982

Two Beautiful

In the very early years of my photography career, I took part time jobs here or there to pay the bills. Sometimes I filled in at a camera shop, selling equipment, processing film, restocking shelves or assisting on location shoots.

They were mostly male photographers then, so I'd fetch coffee, reload film into cameras, hand them lenses, adjust lighting and other gopher duties and sometimes I was second camera for the more senior photographers for additional shots. I was already a damn good photographer in my own right, but everyone has to pay their dues when they're coming up in the business. I didn't mind. I was learning more doing this hands on work than I could have ever learned sitting in a photography class reading about the art.

On the location shoots, we did family portraits, baby pictures, graduation photos, engagement photos and headshots for business publications. Part of my job as assistant was putting the clients at ease and fixing hair that was unruly, or tucking in a stray strap, smoothing a wedding gown and titling a head just so as the guys called out instructions from behind their viewfinders. I enjoyed knowing that moving that one piece of hair away from a bride's mouth where it had stuck in her lip gloss insured that she would, forever, have a beautiful picture of this special day.

I'd been assisting for Bill on odd jobs for more than a year and he came to me with a sheepish look. "What, exactly, is *that* look on your face?" I teased him.

"I've got a job this weekend and I need an assistant. You're the best, Pan."

"Thanks, buddy. So, what's the catch? Tell me this isn't a zoo shoot where I have to wrangle alligators for the camera, because they freak the hell out of me."

"No. No alligators. It's nothing like that. It's … well, it's not your average photo shoot. It pays a bundle, but the couple…well…"

"The couple well…what, Bill?"

"Well, um, they'll be au natural."

"Naked? They want you to photograph them naked?"

"Um, yeah. It's a little more than that. They want photographs of them while they're, uh… um…"

"Having sex? They want you to photograph them naked and having sex. Right?" I laughed, knowing that this shy man was struggling to tell me the details.

"Yeah. That's the size of it. They want tasteful, as in more Oui and less Hustler, if you know what I mean. Look, if you're offended I apologize. I'd never want to jeopardize our working relationship and I can't afford to lose an assistant as good as you. Just tell me to drop it if you don't want to do it."

"I'm in."

"Really? Just like that?"

"Look Bill, There's not much I haven't seen before and, hell, I was a life art class model for petty cash back in school and if I can sit naked in a room with 20 college kids staring at my nipples, I think I can handle seeing a couple of naked people doing the deed."

"Ok, great. You're a real trooper, Pan. It's Saturday night and I'll leave you the address. We're shooting at their house up on Mountain View. I'll bring the gear with me so you can just meet me there."

As the weekend approached, I found myself wondering what this couple would be like. They were probably past middle aged, a fairly attractive woman and not so much for the guy. Whatever. I'd be taking home a healthy pay-check that would cover a couple of bills, so that's what counted.

On Saturday, I wound my way up the mountain road, high up into the hills. The address came into view on one of those glow signs that sit low on the roadside in these affluent neighborhoods. I pulled up to the gate and rang the buzzer. A woman's voice came over the intercom and after I gave my name, the electric gate swung slowly open and I drove my car up the long drive to the main entrance.

I was impressed with the Spanish style mansion tucked up here on the hillside, but my jaw dropped when I was led by the housekeeper, into the great room and with its sweeping vista on the valley below. Floor to ceiling windows opened out to the city with lights twinkling and no neighbors were to be seen from any angle. Millions, I thought, this house must be worth millions.

Bill arrived a moment later and a man in his mid thirties came towards us from the hallway. He was handsome, tall and lean and his tanned body was covered in a gauze shirt, left open, showing his muscular abs and chest and a pair of gauzy beach pants that floated just above his bare feet. Not what I was expecting. Way better.

Bill introduced me to our client, Phillip. We shook hands and Phillip turned to the house keeper and dismissed her for the night.

"Please. Bring your things and follow me." His voice was deep and clear with a soft French accent. As we made our way down the long tiled hallway we chatted about Lyon, where he had grown up. We arrived at a set of glass stairs that seemed to be floating out of the wall and we descended to the lower level of the house.

Here, we found what must be their version of a casual living room. The thirty foot wide space was a sea of white sofas, pillows, sheepskin rugs and white ceramic vases that held dozens of white calla lilies. It was stunning.

I asked Phillip how he wanted us to manage the bounced light from the glass windows if we were using the city view as a back drop. I would have hated drawing the drapes on that view to avoid flash glare. He handed me a remote control, showing me how to start the glass walls moving off to either side of the room. This left the warm summer night air moving in and the smell of jasmine from the balcony wall filled my nostrils. It was an intoxicating space. Soft, sensual music filled the room from their sound system and before I started swaying to a samba, I broke my reverie and got back to work.

We set up our cameras and I loaded film and lined them up as I usually did in easy reach if we needed a lens change or a specialty filter. I lit candles around the room for a softer light effect. We moved our bounce lights into position so that wherever we would be shooting, we had shadows only if we wanted them.

I held a long lens in my left hand and screwed the bayonet mount onto a camera. The side door opened and Lily came into the room. I might have been breathing, then again, maybe not. She was at least 5'10" and her long flowing hair was copper and fire reaching all the way down to her perfect and shapely ass. She had ice green eyes and her bowed mouth was painted a shade of red made famous by Revlon in the glamour girl era of Hollywood. Phillip walked up behind her and sensually moved her hair away from her neck and planted a gentle kiss at her collar bone. His eyes met mine as he said, "This iz my beautiful Lily. I don't wan a pornography movie. I wan still shots of heat and beauty. You can see why I want a photographic record of her, no?"

Lily wore a sheer, floor length peignoir, white, like the room. Beneath it I could see a white lace demi bra and matching lace panties that rode high on her hips and dipped down to her pubic bone in the front. Her white high heels made her calf muscles look fabulous. This might prove to be more difficult than I thought it would be since I could already feel moisture and a little pulse between my own legs after seeing these two perfect human specimens.

I truly love the human body. It is art and grace combined and I can appreciate the exquisite beauty of both the male and female form. Even strictly straight women would moisten up involuntarily at the sight of this couple, and Lily in particular.

"Yes. I understand. You are very beautiful, Lily"

"Thanks, darlin. You're a juicy thing yourself." Her Texas twang was a surprise, but then this whole night was surprising.

"We begin? Yes?" Phillip asked.

They wanted some pictures in varying states of undress and they wanted to be posed. "Pan?" Lily called, "Honey, why don't you come over here and position us for the camera. Make me look fabulous for my lover. "

I hoped the heat in my face wasn't so obvious that it stopped me from being professional. It had long been a fantasy of mine to be able to direct erotic photo scenes using the most perfect elements available.

I crossed over to the two of them and after a moment of thought, I had Phillip sit down on the sofa and Lily stand in front of him. I had him take off his shirt so we could see that perfect chest and I placed her hands on his knees so she was bending forward. "May I?" I asked, indicating her clothing. "Sugar, I am your dress up doll tonight. Do whatever you want with me."

I gave a smile and opened her peignoir coat and swept the sheer fabric over the far half of her rear end so the camera could catch her gorgeous legs and perfect ass cheek from the side. I grabbed her copper hair and floated it down her back with a few strands falling over her creamy exposed cheek. I moved her shoulders back and her chest forward, towards Phillip, while her demi-bra did its job of mounding those perfect breasts up. With the main camera on her left, I positioned her right shoulder slightly forward so her cleavage would shadow and highlight the décolletage. I took Phillips left hand and had him cup Lily's right breast and moved his face towards hers for a kiss.

The moment just before contact is like a match lighting a fuse and I knew it would look spectacular on film.

Bill's camera fired away as they kissed and when I told Phillip to slide the right breast out of the bra, lick his lips and move slowly towards her nipple. Lily said, "Ooo. I like this girl, Phillip. Can we keep her?" Bill caught every second before Phillips lips pressed onto the pink flesh and on to a suck and release that made me secretly do a kegel. He slid both her breasts out of their lace traps and continued to delicately savor her now erect nipples while the camera clicked away.

Next I moved them to Lily standing while Phillip was on his knees in front of her. The camera had a good line across his muscular back and his nicely shaped rear end was defined through the gauze pants. I guided his hand to slide into the side of her panties with his fingers splayed across the lace at her crotch and a thumb disappearing into the folds of her pussy. I had Lilly toss her hair back as he did this and his thumb work made her moan.

"Hold onto your breasts now Lily. Raise them up so that delicious cleavage is even more pronounced. Yes, like that. Bill, is this working?"

"Yeah Pan. It's working." I heard the motor drive clicking away next to me and when I looked over at Bill, his eye to the viewfinder, I couldn't help but notice the prominent bulge in his pants. So did Lily.

"Ooo. You like this Bill?" she said playfully.

"It's great. We're getting great stuff," he replied, trying to sound in control.

"And you Pan?" Lily asked. "Do you like what you see?"

"If I could have a visible hard on right now, you'd have your answer. Suffice it to say this is very hot. Are you two ready to move to something else now?"

We changed a few lenses and I loaded more film in the cameras and then I had Phillip stand up and I slid his gauze pants down. Adjusting them for the shot and since he was going commando, I had a front row seat to his lovely cock. I had moved the pants down just to his beautiful tanned and toned thighs, making his member available for Lily. I had Lily in her bra and panties, shoes on, and kneeling in front of Philip, I had her place her hands flat on his thighs and moved her mouth to within an inch of his waiting cock. The hot shot again was just before the contact. I put her hands onto his rock hard ass and made her press her red nails into his skin and we captured the pressure marks from her fingers, still red when she slid them away. I had Lily lift one foot, giving the shot a campy pinup air, which she loved.

"Bill, can you do some long shots here and then can we get close up for something special." He obliged. I had already set the close up camera on a short tripod and I moved it over to frame the scene.

"Lily, I want your mouth really wet and you're going to have to suck on him a bit so his cock is slick for the camera. OK?" She nodded and gathered some saliva and pressed her beautiful red lips around his eager cock. The camera clicked away and she moved her head back and forth taking him in and out.

"OK. Now Lily, I want you to very slowly open your lips and slide your tongue along the shaft until just the tip of your tongue is touching the head." I had placed some candles on the floor on the other side of them and the light shimmered through the wetness. "Now, very, very slowly, with your tongue still out move it away from the head." And there was the money shot; a shimmering string of saliva connecting her tongue to Phillips cock like the first spin of a spider's web. This is how we catch them, I thought, on a sex web they don't want to leave.

"Did you get that Bill? The saliva?" Bill was having a hard time breathing but he managed a nod.

I knew Lily's perfect ass would be something we needed to memorialize on film. After we took a short break, I had her turn, ass towards the camera and bending forward holding onto her ankles. They must do yoga because both Phillip and Lily were very flexible and strong. She still wore her panties, bra and those sky high heels. I moved her hair around on the floor to fan it out and adjusted her panties so just a bit of her labial lips were showing. She gave a tiny sigh as my fingers brushed her sensitive crotch. The fine line of copper curly hair framed the glorious red, engorged now from the excitement of the shoot and the heat she was feeling being watched, filmed and eventually fucked for an adoring audience. We got some shots of just Lily in that classic submissive pose and then I moved Phillip in, naked now to unwrap his present.

Bill got shots as the panties were slid over her ass and down Lily's long legs revealing her glistening pussy to the camera. I had Phillip lift one of her legs from the fabric but I made him leave the panties around her other ankle. I moved the close up camera for Bill and positioned it at an angle to be able to catch Phillips tongue make its descent to the juicy destination in front of him. "Ok, Phillip. Just like Lily did, let's have you go very slowly and contact the tip of your tongue to the ruffles near her clit. Yeah, just like that." The camera was clicking. "Now slowly, bury your tongue in her and then bring it all the way out again." He did with sounds of pleasure. Lily was sighing and moaning through the shoot and raising the heat level in the room exponentially.

"Now flatten your tongue and I want a slow lick from the top of her slit all the way up to her lower back. Go really wet and really slow. Perfect! Damn, I can't wait for you to see how hot this looks!" As his tongue glided towards Lily's perfect bud anus, Philip ducked his tongue in making Lily buck.

"Sugar, I'm gonna lose it here. I need to cum, now!" she cried.

I took the close up camera off the tripod and Bill went back to the long lens again. Unbeknownst to me, he got some shots of me on my knees and leaning towards all that flesh while photographing Lily & Phillip.

"All right you two. Go for it." Phillip went back to Lily's pussy and began to lick and suck in earnest. Lily was propped with one hand down on the floor and was pinching her own nipple with the other hand while Phillip continued to dine on her lovely cunt. She gave a huge shudder when she came, covering Phillips already wet mouth with her juice. He got to his feet , grabbed her hips and buried his cock inside her while my close up camera caught his stiff shaft sinking and rising and glistening in candlelight, as he pumped her soundly.

I was very wet and turned on by the show going on two feet from me but I kept the camera level and just got into following the slapping sound and wet sucking noises his cock was making inside her. He finally came and before he slid out I made him move slowly again to see the removal and the wet evidence of their sex.

Lily went to freshen up and Phillip pulled his gauze pants back on while Bill and I started to break down the gear. Bill had the bags on his shoulder and was saying goodbye when I heard Lily call from the other room for me to come in for a minute. Phillip said he would walk him out and I told Bill I'd see him back at the studio on Monday and turned towards Lily's voice.

I stepped through what I thought was a master bedroom door, but was apparently just a guest room. Lily was standing with one foot up on a chair and doing a quick wipe of her pussy with a wet cloth.

She strutted over to me, tall and gorgeous and naked and still in those damn high heels. Without any fanfare, while looking me straight in the eyes, she glided her perfectly manicured hand into my pants to touch my wetness. A very wicked smile spread across her mouth, "Oh yes. You did like that. I thought you did. So, Sugar, how about another evening with just you, me and your camera sometime soon? I'll make it very memorable." For emphasis, she moved her fingers on my clit until I gasped.

"What would Phillip say about all this?" My voice was shaky from her finger work.

She brought her hand out of my pants and put her fingers in her mouth. Then she leaned forward and pressed her red lips on mine and used her tongue, wet with my own juice, to circle my open lips.

With a playful kiss she said, "Well, darlin, who do think is going to be taking the pictures?"

We exchanged numbers and agreed we would set a date for a second, more private session the following week.

"The difference between pornography and erotica is lighting."

Gloria Leonard

Chapter 9

Los Angeles 1982

Let's See What Develops

What a world of difference photography is today compared to when I started. With the arrival of digital cameras, anyone with even a modicum of vision and one good eye can now create some amazing photos. With the addition of Photoshop and other editing software, a bad shot can be reworked into one far better and people with all sorts of flaws can be made flawless with a snip here and a brush there. I get it. It's immediately satisfying to see your work seconds after you shoot, but digital photography killed the romance of film photography and completely did away with the magical tension and delayed pleasure of a darkroom. As I look now, at some of the prints from that memorable shoot, the perfection of the subjects could never have been improved with any new photographic software. They were, they are, perfect.

A few days after what would turn out the be the first of many intimate photo shoots in my life, I found myself in the studio darkroom working my way through batches of wedding and graduation prints that were rush ordered by other clients.

It took a couple of days to clear the big stack of work that had accumulated on my desk. Late summer was always a busy time for us. Since they weren't in a hurry for their prints, when I finally got my hands on the film from Phillip & Lily's shoot, I was re-energized and eager to get going. I ran them through the processer solution and did the stabilizer and rinse and stretched like a cat as my back was stiff from so many hours in the darkroom. When I finally pulled the film out to hang for drying, I had to sneak a peek at the strips while they hung there on the wire.

Small captures of those smooth bodies danced in the darkroom fan breeze and I breathed a sigh of relief to know that every roll was perfect. I had a couple of hours before I could make a contact sheet so I headed out for lunch while I had the time. I carried the other finished work with me as I made my way back out to the main studio where Bill was holding down the fort. I handed them off to him with a cursory run through of which jobs were done and he offered to bag them and call the clients in to pick up the finished proofs or select enlargements from the thumbnail samples I'd printed.

"Bill, I just hung the Brevard's negs to dry and I'll print some contact pages after lunch ok?"

"Great. That's great. Did they all make it?"

"Yep. Every juicy one." I quipped. Bill was a happily, faithfully married man and a pretty quiet one at that. It had surprised me that he'd taken on a job like the Brevard's, but with a house mortgage and two teenagers heading to college in a few years, money was money and photos were photos.

"That was…uh…really something. Huh?" It's about as much in depth on the topic as he was going to go and not wanting to haul him through an embarrassing conversation I just agreed and headed out the door on my break.

I ran some errands and finally sat down for a bit to enjoy my salad and fresh lemonade at the café around the corner. When I was ready I made my way back to the studio. Bill was talking to a mom and her cheerleader daughter about the graduation portrait sitting they were about to shoot. He didn't need my help so I went back to the darkroom.

Cranking up my music to keep me company as I worked, I laid the negative strips out and printed up contact pages first. When they were ready, I grabbed a loupe and had a closer look. It was magazine quality, stunning, erotic and off the hot scale by a mile. Though the photos were in color, I picked my three favorites and just for the hell of it, I decided to print some enlargements in classic black and white on matte archival paper.

With so many pictures to choose from I had a hard time narrowing the choices down to just three. By the time I selected them I was feeling a little twingey in my nethers with all that glorious skin in my face again. These two were born to be on film and I felt a little more than proud that we had captured so intimate a relationship between this god and goddess on film.

I ran the 11 X 14 paper through the developer, the stop bath and the fixer. I did a permawash and rinse and with my fingers, gingerly pulled the paper out of the bath and turned it around. There, in all their glory was Phillip's beautiful mouth pulling away from Lily's perfect nipple, her poreless skin, even blown up to this size photo and the wetness of their contact shimmered on the paper. I felt a tight pull in my crotch as I gazed at the whispery fine hairs on her skin and the look of pure devotion on Phillip's face.

The second was another 11 X 14 of Lily with her tongue near Phillips stiff cock. Again, the texture of their skin and the heat of the moment made an incredibly sexy combination. For the last enlargement, I picked one of the shots where I had Lily bending over and holding her ankles. We were still setting up the shot and she had swung her head back to look at me while I was giving her directions and I fired off a few shots. Her long hair had naturally swept out around her like a fire curtain from her motion and those legs that just kept going rose from her white high heels all the way up to that perfect peak of her perfect ass. The city lights in the back ground and candlelight flickering on the edges of the frame created a breath taking photograph.

I set the three enlargements hanging on the wire to air and I rolled my chair over to the door to throw the lock in case Bill or someone else wandered back there. Here with my own private showing of this sensual art photography laid out before me, I couldn't resist a little celebratory jilling off.

Over in my hand bag, I had one of my little quiet vibrator toys that I'd picked up earlier on my lunch break from the adult toy store in town. I pulled it out of the bag and lifting my cotton sundress and brought the little devil down to my pulsing clit while I feasted my eyes on the photos of the beautiful Phillip and Lily. I turned up the power and while I relived in my mind's vagina some of the hotter moments of the photo shoot, I climaxed hard right there in the dark room with Bill and mom and cheerleader daughter just 30 feet away and unaware.

After I'd cooled off, I picked up the phone and dialed the number on Lily's elegant calling card.

"Hello?" Her silky voice matched the rest of her.

"Lily? It's Pandora from Valley Art Photography."

"Honey, it's delicious Pandora." I heard her call out to wherever Phillip was.

"I've got some contact sheets for you to look at from your session and… I hope you don't mind, but I took the liberty of making you a few special prints."

"Fabulous! How about you come on over for dinner tomorrow… let's say eight… and you can bring them with you then. Would that be all right for you, Sugar?"

"Uh, sure. That sounds like a plan."

"I am so looking forward to this." She breathed into the phone before she quickly added, "Pandora, do you eat seafood?"

"Seafood. Yes. I love seafood. So I will see you at 8 to-morrow then?"

"Eight. Can't wait. Bye now." The line went quiet and it took me a moment to catch my breath. What else did this Venus have on the menu? I had a feeling it was going to be me.

*"It's not true that I had nothing on.
I had the radio on."*

Marilyn Monroe

Chapter 10

Los Angeles 1982

The Lily Session

I was already at my door with the photo package under my arm when I stopped and turned back to my room. I peeled off my clothing and replaced the standard under-garments with black lace panties and a leather bustier and pulled my jeans back on. I tossed a loose boyfriend sweater over the leather just in case I was being presumptuous about the possibility of sex. The sweater wouldn't look so eager. Besides, it isn't always about what everyone else sees on the outside that makes you feel like a bombshell, it's the secret, hidden parts that make you burn.

I had slipped a dab of pheromone perfume between my breasts because it always makes me a little giddy to smell it and grabbing my jacket, the photos and the bottle of white wine, I almost skipped out to my car.

When I got to the Brevard's gate, the housekeeper let me in and I parked my car out front where I had the week prior for our photo shoot. Lily met me at the door in a teal cotton sundress and her hair swept into a loose braid that only a hairdresser could have made that casually elegant. She had fine silver chain earrings with sparkles of amethyst dangling at the ends and they moved as she pulled me into a hug and, to my surprise, planted a kiss onto my mouth in greeting. Phillip arrived and with typical French style, kissed both my cheeks and put out his hands to accept the wine gift and photo package from me.

They swept me into the upstairs living room and we settled onto a large sofa looking out on the city. Phillip opened the photo package pulled out the contact sheets and the loupe I had provided so they could get a better look at the small thumbnail prints. I reached to the table for the other part of the package and handing them to Phillip, said, "I hope you don't mind. I couldn't resist making these for you two."

He raised his eye brow adding "Hmm. What have we here?" He slipped his hand under the brown paper wrapping to bring out the three enlargements I had made. He sucked in a slow breath and Lily gasped as she saw the three prints laid out side by side on the glass coffee table.

"Oh my God. I am going to cry."

"Oh, Jeez! I'm sorry! Should I have not done this?"

"No, no, no. You don't understand, dear. These are the most beautiful pictures I've ever seen. I look amazing! Phillip! I can't believe it? Can you believe it?"

"Yes, darling. I do believe it. This iz you! This iz how I see you all the time," he cooed.

"Oh phew! For a moment, I thought you didn't like them and I'd screwed this up big time." I was relieved.

"Pan, these are exquisite. You have captured my beautiful Lily, her heat and her passion, for all time. Thank you so much." He squeezed my hand and Lily kissed my cheek.

We spent a little time looking through the contact sheets and commenting on some of the other pictures and Phillip said he had a projection system they could use on a large screen to go through them more thoroughly.

The house keeper came to the door and softly said that dinner was ready and I noticed her eyes glance over to the table where her employers' lovely cock was immortalized on film. She blushed and turned back towards the kitchen.

"Thank you, Rose. That will be all for tonight. We'll get these things later. Have a good night." Lily dismissed the housekeeper and we made our way to the table laden with dozens of dishes and over flowing flower arrangements.

"Wow. This is quite a spread! Are there more people joining us?"

"No, honey, I wasn't sure what you'd like so I had Rose make a little of everything." Lily purred.

There were crab claws and lobster tail, gigantic Guaymas shrimp and even an ice bowl with oysters and mussels and lemon slices. The spicy sauces and the three types of salads went perfectly with the champagne Phillip poured for us all. We filled our plates from the buffet and they led me out to the terrace where we ate under the stars. We spoke about art and photography in particular, then music and Europe and how the two of them had met. It was a lovely meal and good conversation and the champagne had me very relaxed. By the time Lily brought out some chocolate covered strawberries and held one to my mouth for a bite, my head was resting back on the chair and I was drinking in the night.

She stood behind my chair with her soft hands on my neck, her thumbs gently rubbing away tension. She purred into my ear that Phillip was her one and only man and she was his one and only woman, but sometimes, she wanted a woman for herself and Phillip loved to watch all that female energy. She asked me to make love with her while Phillip observed us and took some photos for their private collection.

I tilted my head back and drew her down to my mouth for a kiss that was hidden by her loosening braid.

"Are you sure you're OK with this, Phillip?" I asked.

"Oh yes, Cherie. Theez iz one of my most favorite things, to watch two beautiful females bring each other pleasure. Every man loves theez but not many have ever seen theez wonder in the flesh. I am a very lucky man. Please, Cherie, devour my wife."

We rose from the table and Lily took my hand and led me to their master suite. An enormous bed waited there, covered in soft cashmere throws. Lily led me to the middle of the room while Phillip brought his camera out and started to quietly move around us, returning the favor snapping pictures of us like I had done of him and his wife. Lily pulled my sweater off and seeing my leather bustier she sucked in a breath and ran her hands up my sides. She unzipped my pants and had me step out of them, revealing the black lacey front thong panties. "What size shoes do you wear Pan?"

"9 1/2 medium."

"Wait right here!" She disappeared behind a louvered screen and I heard another door open into what may have been a second room. It was either that or a ridiculously big closet. I'm guessing the later. When she came back around the screen looking triumphant, she was dangling a pair of four inch heeled black patent leather fuck me shoes in one hand and had an ankle length mink coat draped on a finger over her shoulder.

"These," she said like a sorority sister, "are for you." She handed me the shoes. "And this…" She spread the coat out across the bed, mink side up. "…is for us." She sat on the bed and smoothed her whole arm length across the fur and patted it.

I was standing in my panties and the leather bustier and I picked up one foot and then the other as I slid the dangerous looking shoes onto my feet. I looked down at them and did a small twirl to show her how they looked and she let out a soft sound. "You look good enough to eat, Miss Pandora."

I did a slow cat walk to the bed and turned my head towards Phillip for a moment. He was smiling and watching us while shooting pictures from his cozy corner of the room. Lily rolled off the bed and went to a side table where she took a gold box out of the top drawer.

My mind was racing wondering what she had planned. Handcuffs or a whip or some electronic toy could be moments away from tender parts of my anatomy. The anticipation was frustrating and exciting in equal measures. She carried it back to the bed and asked me to sit with my legs crossed, lotus style in the middle. I obliged and she crawled up on the bed and sat just behind me.

Here we go. I felt her hands remove the clip from my hair and she let it fall down my back. The next sensation surprised me even more. She took a boar bristle brush and started to slowly brush my hair out. That was unexpected. What a luxurious feeling it is to have someone brush your hair for you. I sighed. No equipment tonight; just our very own bodies and our imaginations.

"That's right, baby. Just relax and let me take care of you." Lily purred while she brushed. After several lingering moments, she set the brush down and scooted over next to me dragging the gold box with her.

She took my face in her hands and turned it right and left, inspecting it. Out came an array of makeup, mostly things I don't typically wear. With my eyes closed, she worked carefully to apply shadows and liners and coats of mascara. I already had a small beauty mark on my left cheek and she used a pencil to darken it. She dusted a shimmering powder over my cheeks while cooing about how gorgeous this or that was.

Phillip had moved his viewing position over closer and when she tilted my head back and applied a wild reddish pink color to my lips, he snapped a few photos and complimented Lily on her masterful eye. With a soft and small paint brush, she dipped it into a pot of slick gloss and covered my now red lips. It's a sealer so you're smudge proof."

She put the box down on the floor. "All done. Come with me." She put out her hand to take mine and held it close as I followed her to the makeup table chair on the other side of the louvered screen. She motioned for me to sit and she clicked on the surrounding mirror lights and I saw what she had done.

Instead of passably pretty me, there was a sultry knock-out looking back. My eyes were surrounded with dark shadow and lined in black that curved just slightly at the outer corners. It made my olive hazel eyes jump out. And my red lips were thick and pouty and looked positively sinful. I've never seen my face done up like a femme fatale and after being amazed, I reached back to Lily who was standing behind me and pulled her around and onto my lap so I could look at our faces together in the mirror.

Our cheeks were pressed side by side and Phillip's camera was clicking away somewhere behind us. "Look at how dark and delicious you are. You're looking like a dangerous assassin on a mission in Berlin." Lily was cooing.

She reached over and unlaced my leather bustier just enough for the front to fall open and show the edges of my nipples. She stepped back behind me and with her long fiery hair sliding over one of my shoulders she told me to look at myself as she brought her mouth to my neck and started a run of kisses and trailing her tongue along it. Phillip had shrugged out of his shirt now and I could see him behind us angling his camera and recording every lick. His cotton pants were straining in the front as he watched his beautiful wife touching this dark and mysterious stranger.

She slid her hand around and into the top of my bustier and pinched when she found my nipples. My legs were spreading of their own accord and a moment later Lily took my hand again to bring me back to the bed.

"Phillip, the mirror please." He pushed a button somewhere and I heard a sliding sound above the bed and a border of small lights came on around the canopy. At the edge of the bed she reached to her shoulders to untie her sundress and let it fall to the floor. She was wearing a bright raspberry pink strapless bra and matching panties and still looking at me, she crawled backwards until she was lying on the mink she had spread out earlier. "Come to me", she purred.

I stalked over her until I was hovering just above her body and I reached with one hand behind her head and pulled her into a steamy wet kiss. Our lips moved like velvet against each other. It's such a different sensation from kissing a man. Even when you kiss her hard, it's still a very female thing. We twined our tongues together and I lingered there a moment tasting her beautiful mouth.

"Oooo, that was lovely Pan." She put her arms around me and smoothly flipped me onto my back.

"This mink just feels like sex," I said. When I looked up, I saw a mirror as large as the bed and Lily's perfect ass reflected there as she moved up on me on hands and knees.

"Do you like my mirror, Sugar? It's such a fabulous view, I think." She giggled.

"I couldn't agree more. I have to confess that when I finished printing those pictures of you the other day, I had to pull out my vibrator because you made me so hot just seeing your ass again."

"That's so sexy to know I made you come without even being there." She looked towards Phillip and licked her lips.

Pulling on the string of my bustier, Lily had it off me in moments and her hands were caressing my breasts. Lipstick on nipples is a thing of beauty. She pulled them up and pinched and rolled licked my sensitive nipples and when she had them just the right shade of red and puckered to perfection, she brought her mouth down and sucked with all her might. I cried out and I'm sure some juice spilled out of me. Lily gave the same attention to the other breast and then started planting kisses and a trail of red lipstick down my stomach.

I was watching us in the over head mirror. When she reached my mound, she slid her hands under the strings of my thong and worked it off me leaving me naked except for the fuck me shoes. I was lying sprawled across the decadent mink surface that caressed every inch of me. I just had to move around to feel the fur and Lily was laughing as she watched me. She moved like a cat up my legs and used her forearms to push them open so my freshly shaved pussy was on display. She licked her full lips and lowered them down until she was giving my clit a series of sucks. Just when her motion started to build a fire in my cunt, she changed to her tongue. Never be fooled. Men can learn to perform cunnilingus very well, but women are experts. We know our bodies better than anyone.

She licked and tickled with her long fingernails along the ruffles of my labia, then she would dive in again and pull a half dozen sucks out of me. I watched her plunging two fingers into my wet cave while her tongue continued to play across my clit and it sent my back arching up and my ass rising off the bed. I was caressing my breasts and my climax was building until I couldn't hold back any longer. I dug the heels of my black shoes into the bed and cried out, my head snapping back like I'd been hit with a sucker punch. I dropped back down on the bed and sighed and laughed and sighed again. "Amazing ... completely amazing. " That's all I could get out while I recovered my breath.

Lily grabbed the glasses of wine that Phillip had put on the nightstand, handing the second to me. I took a drink and asked Phillip if he would mind bringing the photos in that I had brought them earlier. When he returned, I set the three oversized prints up by the head board of the bed so Lily could see them while I took my turn.

I took Lily by the hand and had her stand at the foot of the bed, so she could see the photos in front of her. "Look at you, Lily. You're a goddess; all silk and fire. You're so beautiful." I whispered into her ear. I slowly removed her bra and panties while Phillip took more pictures. I noticed that this time, she had also shaved her pussy bare, just like mine. Maybe she'd decided to surprise me after reaching into my pants the other day and discovering the silken hairless flesh. I was intrigued. "This is nice Lily. I love the way this looks on you," I purred and ran a flat hand over her smooth mound. Now, both of us standing and naked, I pulled her into my arms in a full body embrace pussy to pussy, breast to breast. I kissed her juicy mouth with such heat that she was winding her hands through my hair and wrapping a leg around my body so I could feel her high heel pressing into me. I brought her nipples, one at a time, into my painted mouth. And she let out a note of excitement when I sucked as hard as she had. Women let you know what they want done to their bodies by the way they handle yours and Lily wanted to feel that connection between nipple and clitoris in a powerful way.

I moved her feet apart and made sure she held the tension in her legs. Any sort of restraint or just having to hold tension in your body while someone is arousing you, heightens the pleasure of release. I knelt down on the floor and grabbed her ass bringing her pussy to my mouth to return the favor she had done for me earlier. My tongue licked and lapped and I used the same pulsing suck technique that she had used on my clit. I could feel her waves of excitement as the tension built in her perfect body.

I pulled away for a moment, juicy lipped and asked, "Phillip, is it against the rules if you come over here and fuck your wife from behind while I continue what I'm doing?"

"Cherie, she can reach a climax many times. Bring her to full pleasure theez time. When you arouse her again and bring her close to orgasm, I will go to her then. I must see her face theez wonze."

I did as I was told and added some fingers into her wet pussy. Taking some of her juice along, I plunged another finger into her anus and she rocked backwards and forward. I licked and pumped my fingers until she screamed in ecstasy and her knees buckled.

"Oh, good lord. I came so hard I thought I was gonna black out!" We were laughing as she dropped down to the floor where I was sitting now and kissed and licked her own juice off my face.

When she had recovered a bit, I told her we weren't done yet and I pulled her back up onto the bed and positioned her on her hands and knees near the bottom edge of the bed. I playfully licked and sucked my way under her until my face was positioned just below her glorious pussy and hers was over mine.

She dropped her painted red lips down to my wet pussy as I brought mine up to hers and we pleasured our way together matching lick for lick and suck for suck. When she was starting to shake, I waved Phillip over and he brought a lubricant with him. Smearing a generous amount on his cock, I watched as he added more to his hand and circled Lily's anus with it, working a finger in her delicate bud to loosen her. He set his throbbing cock just outside her small puckered hole and I reached up and sunk my fingers into her pussy as he began to thrust into her ass. Lily was overwhelmed with her mouth busy on my pussy and the double pleasure of having her cunt filled with my fingers and her ass with her husband's hard, slippery cock.

In a moment, she abandoned my cunt and was calling out "Yes! Yes! Don't stop! I'm almost there! Yes!" a crescendo of body wracking orgasms hit Lily and Phillip and my own pussy was humming in the afterglow.

We stayed like that, the three of us, for a few moments and when Phillip pulled out of Lily, a stream of cum poured onto my hair and face. "Oh, I am so sorry, Pan." He said, and I laughed.

Lily brought me to her shower and she washed my hair and took off my makeup and towel dried me like a doll. She insisted I take the shoes as a gift for the photo enlargements. It was sweet and sexy and a perfect ending to this night of burning silken heat with a real live goddess.

Though I've never used their real names, I've shared this story on occasion with a lover or a friend and it has come to be known amongst those who have heard it as *The Lily Session*. Some doubted that it ever happened. I love to watch their jaw drop when I step into my closet and carry out the shoes.

"Don't worry. It only seems kinky the first time."

Author Unknown

Chapter 11

Laguna Beach 1995

A Matter of Taste

I've been thinking about "firsts" in my life; sex firsts and how that new technique made it into my skill's tool kit in the first place.

We think we've seen and done everything we could do right up until we're wrist deep into something we haven't encountered yet, and then we're knocked back to regroup and process the experience into whatever category this new thing should fall into. Do we love it? Do we hate it? Do we want to do it again, just not with this person?

Michelangelo said, "I am still learning." I'll bet he learned many things while "studying" the model that posed for The David statue, which would explain the fabulous detail of its perfect ass. Sex skills are something we will use for a lifetime, and having some options beyond the standard three or four most people have, will keep you and your partner interested in continuing to get excited about each other. We learn to drive a stick shift or operate some other piece of machinery; we gain some mastery over a cooking technique or learn to surf. There will always be another thing that's waiting out there for us to discover if we're open to change.

In the world of sex and bedroom games, there is always some new thing to discover and the techniques often enter our lives along with the welcoming of a new lover into our beds. Imagine the web of information you'd have if you could map the origins of sex technique. Who taught a lover that particular finger placement and just how to move a tongue that way and in turn who taught their teacher?

I am guessing it would wind its way back to Kali herself, the Hindu mother goddess and destroyer of ignorance. We are ignorant in our innocence until Kali arrives and opens our eyes. We do not know until the moment that we do know. Then, the game changes.

Maybe they saw a new trick in a movie like when Marlon Brando unwittingly became the international spokesperson for butter after Last Tango in Paris. Maybe they heard about it in the locker room when a team mate bragged about their latest conquest. Maybe their old lover sprang it on them during makeup sex and recognizing it as something new, it led to another breakup over the affair where they'd learned it.

With new lovers, there's a delicate dance between ooh-La-la and what the fuck. Discovering where the line between too much and not enough, safe zone or are we pushing the boundaries could mean we risk exposing ourselves and our preferences and we risk shifting their perception of us forever. Our skill sets are a collection of favorite hits from everyone we have ever known, and finding a new lover who has some matching skills and preferences may be rarer than you might think. Our personal tastes are

widely varied. Just look at the choices in an American grocery store's cereal aisle! That's just breakfast food and there
are hundreds of choices. What you like to have happen to
your body is even more individualized.

I remember the first time a man had me get up from a
missionary position and bent me over the edge of the bed
to take me from behind. I was young and inexperienced
and had no idea what he was about to do but he was a dan-
gerously attractive man and we found ourselves locked in a
little sex tornado for a few days while he was visiting town.
It was my first time with him and though we had managed one round in the missionary plank mode, he wanted
to have me this new way. It took about two minutes to
figure out that in this position, with him behind me, that
he could penetrate much deeper and, for me there was a
hundred times more pleasure as his cock hit the front of
my vagina more consistently. He grabbed a hand full of
my hair (another first) and with his other hand he held a
firm grip on my waist as he pulled me back towards him. It
was a revelation to me and I assumed that the other times
I'd had sex, the guys were holding out on me, trying not to
be too wild and scare me off. Silly me.

A few months after that encounter, I had a surprise visit
from Aidan, the one that popped my cherry a few years
earlier. He stayed in my bed that night, a first for us, as we
were previously sniper lovers, quick shots and off we'd go
to our separate lives with none of this girlfriend/boyfriend
sleepover stuff to mess up our arrangement.

We were into our first half hour of heated sex and I
asked him if he would get behind me and he freaked out.
Apparently, my hot play pal was only hot for missionary
sex and I had just asked for something he imagined only

happened with hookers. Granted, we were still in our late teens, so our experience was limited, but the reaction from him was like a slap in the face as the full scope of his innocence arrived in my awareness. It was our last time together and it closed out our history on a rather sour note. I could only imagine that soon after that he would discover other positions on his own and he might feel like an idiot for making such a big deal out of my trying to enlist his enthusiasm for what I felt was a delightful new activity. Maybe the fact that he was the one who had changed my virgin status made him feel that even 2,000 miles away at college, he should have been kept in the loop regarding my sexual knowledge base. Had his virgin moved on to the big kids table without him?

Given that sort of reaction to asking for something different, it's easy to see why we get a bit gun shy with a new sex partner. I have no idea if we're treading on new ground or if it might be a favorite of theirs as well. Every time someone braves the private information abyss and finds a willing play partner, there is a sense of relief that what we like is "normal" and it emboldens us to talk freely and to experiment freely with this new lover.

Benjamin was never shy about what he wanted in the bedroom or anywhere else in his life. He just laid it out in plain language and I would either go along with the request or he would reach into his very deep bag of tricks and pull out something else he had always wanted to try with me. I long suspected that he had an ongoing to do list with notes he'd made from years of letters to Penthouse and Oui. He appeared to be working his way through the list with me and surely his other partners as well.

This particular night, B & I had been locked in a spooning embrace, he laying behind me and pushing from there when he pulled my top leg over his hip to make the front of my body more available and he told me to make myself cum. Up to this moment, all my sexual activities were me doing something to or with someone else or having them done to me. Doing something to myself, well, we had just unlocked the door to a whole new ballroom in this hotel. I actually felt a bit shy about performing this very private ritual in front of someone else even though I'd been observed already from every angle in all sorts of other situations.

He stopped and turned me around when I hesitated and looked me in the eye. "You've never done this before have you? You've never let anyone see you make yourself cum?" I admitted it and he looked very surprised.

"I want you to make yourself cum for me. I want to see how you hold your fingers, how fast or slow you move them and how many you use. I want to see how you keep them slick so they slide on you instead of pull. I want to watch you now. Do it." He had me lay back and he took my hand and put it between my legs.

My eyes were wild and I could feel my breathing quicken for this command performance. I touched tentatively at first and he stretched out next to me stroking my face and my breasts and encouraging me. "That's it. Just reach down and touch like I'm not even here. Close your eyes and just feel what you're doing."

He watched as I plunged two fingers into my wetness and brought them back to my clit and how I held the top part of my pussy open with my other hand. He watched me circle slowly for as long as it took to start building pressure and when I reached again to rewet my fingers, he drew a nipple into his mouth and sucked when I went back to stroking again.

"That's right. I want to see you cum. Keep going. When I watch you like this, I'll know more about what it takes to make you come really hard. That's what I want to be able to do for you. Now I'll know just how long it takes to get you out of control and I can use that when we fuck so I can draw out your pleasure or force you to have a fast, hard orgasm. That's right. Keep stroking until you cum." He was coaching me from the sidelines.

By this time, the idea and embarrassment that he was watching had vanished and I arched my back and brought myself to a shattering orgasm as he guided me along with his words and his tongue.

"That's it baby. You looked amazing just now. Don't be embarrassed. This is going to be a whole new world of fun for us." He was right. We incorporated self play into our sex sometimes and I found out what he already knew, that it added to the pleasure dramatically. When he couldn't reach me from one position or another, he would tell me to touch myself while he stayed in me. What had, one moment before, been foreign territory, was now a normal part of our play.

All was well in the playground of whatever bed we found ourselves on, until we ended our relationship and it left me starting back at the beginning again. With each new lover, we learn anew if their boundaries are far beyond our own or way, way inside the lines that we had already painted with the help of our past lovers.

It's a whole different world in bed when we're comfortable enough to ask our lovers what they want. Bringing a story into the bedroom that includes something you'd like to try creates a safe opportunity to discuss it.

Sometimes, I bring something I've been reading or I ask my lover to read me something that got them hot. You'll never know if you never ask. And who knows, you both may have been holding back on sharing the very same fantasy. Here's how I see it, one of two things will happen; if it's oh-la-la then you're all set for Saturday night and if it's what-the-fuck, then you're probably going to discover a whole lot of other incompatibilities that may be just down the road with this person. Bullet dodged. You're welcome.

Either way, it's a matter of taste, so find out if you both enjoy the same flavors.

"Sex got me into trouble from the age of seventeen. I'm hoping that by the time I'm seventy I'll straighten it out."

Harold Robbins

Chapter 12

Los Angeles 1975

Happy Birthday B

"You've got a birthday coming up this weekend, right?" I asked from the comfy chair where I was writing with my leg draped over the armrest. He was stretched out on the sofa reading the Wall Street Journal.

"Yes, I do. Why do you ask?" He sounded slightly annoyed. Odd, I thought, considering the intimacy of what goes on when we're in bed together, I wondered if I was treading into some sacred ground here that, in his mind, is reserved for a more serious relationship. I had thought we were pretty serious or perhaps, headed that way. A few months back, while shopping in the Galleria, we had passed a jewelry store window filled with rings and he'd slowed to take a look. I'd playfully asked if he needed to know my ring size and he answered with a typically cryptic response, "Possibilities lie within." Why was it so hard for this insanely beautiful man to just say what he meant and not make it sound like a magic eight ball response? I had dearly wanted to shake his head, hard that day, for a different answer.

"If you were free, I was wondering if I could take you on a short getaway, my treat, of course. Catalina maybe or a few days in Santa Barbara or anything else you might want to do."

"Hmm. That's sounds intriguing. You did say anything, correct? Anything I want to do?"

Oh boy. Just how stupid am I to voluntarily give someone like Benjamin, carte blanche? He turned that megawatt face towards my chair and, as it usually was with me and B, the sensation in my panties made my decision for me, but I asked anyway, "Should I be afraid right now?"

He laughed and reached over to my dangling foot and started slowly massaging my instep. "No, Pan. You shouldn't be afraid, just very... very excited."

"OK, what exactly would I be giving you for this birthday gift that's going to excite me?"

"Oh, trust me;" he said with a smirk, "the gift is for me. I just said you'd be excited."

"I'll bite. What's the gift?"

"I want a fantasy … and I want you to agree to star in it…for me."

"Intrigued… what's the fantasy?"

"Ah, well, here's the best part; you won't know until it happens." He began the long slide of his hand up my leg and I huffed out a chuckle and shook my head and he knew he had me.

On Thursday evening, a box arrived by messenger; another of his silver and red satin bow surprises. In the box was a red velvet bustier with lacing up the front. It reminded me of an old West dance hall girl look. Beneath more tissue paper, there was a black garter belt and black stockings and black lace panties. Finally, there was an exquisite strapless black velvet cocktail dress that zipped up the back and a lovely black velvet choker with a dangling garnet heart the size of a quarter hanging from it.

He did love those garters and stockings and I had to admit, after you put them on, they made you walk sexier and talk sexier and act sexier. Win-win I suppose.

The note he had enclosed said, *"The limo will be at your door on Friday, at 8 p.m."* and it was signed in the usual way, "B".

I had often wondered how he managed to orchestrate all the little things he had done during the time I was with him. When we first met, he had arranged to have a single rose waiting on my desk, every morning, for a week. By the end of that first week, I was purring into the phone during his daily calls to check on me and purring into his ear again at night as he brought my body to some Mount Olympus of pleasure.

This birthday gift could either be sweet and romantic or it could be another foray into the bondage and dominance closet he liked to play in sometimes. I was completely enamored with this man and found myself following his every directive just to see how far down the rabbit hole he actually lived while holding out hope that some kind of normal and lasting love would be there waiting for us.

My mind suddenly felt like the scorching Sahara desert. It was hot and blank and emotions started to move on breezes like kicked up sands of thought and settled just as quickly back down to the surface, undistinguishable again from the surrounding sand. I was intrigued, wary, anxious, a dash of fearful and Eros help me, curious.

Beyond the charm and savior faire he offered to the public, he lived at arm's length from any true emotional intimacy. The dichotomy of his invasion of my own privacy and intimate spaces and his guarded and secretive maintenance of his own was very confusing for me, especially at this young age. But I was all in on this E-ticket ride with him.

Friday night, as I waited for the limo to arrive, I smoothed down the side of the cocktail dress. I'll give him this: Benjamin certainly knew how to select clothing that maximized my curves. I felt positively steamy in this dress and the garnet pendant on the choker, cold when I first tied it in place, had now taken on the heat of my body and as it lay in the hollow of my throat, I could feel my pulse just beneath the warm stone.

The limo driver had exited the 110 and was heading down South Figueroa and the Bonaventure Hotel appeared just ahead. He slowed as he pulled up to the front entrance and got out to open my door. I looked around for Benjamin, thinking perhaps he was meeting me for dinner here and had maybe reserved a room for later. Scanning the faces there at the entrance, there was no Benjamin in sight. As I stepped out of the limo, a very attractive young woman in business attire approached the car. "Ms. Bleue?" she inquired.

I nodded and she asked me to please follow her. She quietly led me to the elevator bank and as we road towards the top floors in the glass elevator cab, she simply smiled politely when our eyes met. We exited at a suite level and she indicated that I should turn left. "Right this way, Ms. Bleue. "

"Has Mr. Cutler already arrived?" I asked.

"I've been instructed to bring you here and have you ready for his arrival." Not exactly an answer to my question. Beyond the time and place, I still had no indication about what sort of fantasy gift I had blindly agreed to give to him.

We entered a spacious suite that was elegantly appointed, and from this high up in the building, there was an amazing view of the city below. I saw a table set up for two with champagne already on ice, so perhaps this would be a more romantic adventure...perhaps.

The young woman led me forward to the bedroom area and told me she had specific instructions to follow and then she asked if I needed to use a restroom as this would be a good time to do that. Just to gather my quickly dissolving wits about me, I took her up on the offer and headed towards to enormous bathroom with a Jacuzzi tub that could easily fit two. I took a moment alone to freshen up and to stare in the mirror and wonder just how much I trusted this frustratingly fascinating man after all.

I took a few deep breaths and headed back out to where the woman had waited for me. I could see that she'd made a few "adjustments" to the bed. She had removed the coverlet and the pillows and tied at each corner was a long velvet rope and she had laid the long ends of each rope up on the sheets. She had secured them to the feet on each corner of the bed frame. Innovative, I thought. Even given a simple box frame he could figure out a way to make it more like his iron four poster at his apartment.

OK. It was going to be the other kind of fantasy. I had agreed to this so it was either chicken out or suck it up and play along. "Wow. He's really thought this through." I said aloud, but to myself.

"Mr. Cutler has asked that you remove your dress and panties and I've been instructed to secure you here on the bed. He will be arriving shortly. He has asked that I let you know there will be no painful acts or punishing here tonight and he asks that you continue to trust him."

Wondering where this was all headed, I, once again, let Benjamin, even in his absence, lead me into a deep blue world that I have only visited on occasion.

I momentarily considered stepping back in the rest room to slip out of my velvet dress, but as this woman was about to not only see me partially naked, but in tying the ropes for Benjamin, she would have a view of my vagina that only lovers and my gynecologist get to see, the privacy seemed a bit ridiculous.

I set my dress over a chair and slipped out of the panties and stepped bravely towards the bed. She asked me to sit down had me scoot back enough to be able to get my knees bent. She took a velvet rope and tied one ankle and then the other.

"Please raise your arms up now." she requested. I had lain down and I reached my arms up and she tied the ropes at the head of the bed so that my arms were extended. She was very calm and professional, like she was going to do a simple massage, only I would be restrained and it was just another day for her.

The red velvet bustier had shifted down exposing my breasts above the ruffle of black lace that edged the fabric and the coolness of the room and the heat that was rising in my face as this fantasy started to come to life had me flushed.

"Now, Ms. Bleue, I will be blindfolding you." She took a black velvet blindfold from the side table and tied it over my eyes and asked if it was comfortable. I said it was fine and I could hear her dialing the telephone and she spoke in the receiver, "Yes sir. She's ready. Yes sir, of course." She put the receiver to my ear and I heard Benjamin's voice then. "You're safe. I'm watching you. Just enjoy." Click. The young woman took the phone away and hung it up.

I thought I heard her leave the room and then I heard a sound system come on playing some sort of ambient music throughout the suite. I laid there for a few minutes, arms and legs spread and the air conditioning blowing on my exposed pussy waiting and wondering what was supposed to happen next when the sensation of a tongue dipped in quickly for a lick on my clit.

"Oh! I didn't hear you come in." I said.

"Shhhhhhhhh" Not sure if it was Benjamin's voice, the suspense sent a wave through me like that first steep drop on a roller coaster ride. I was aware of his fantasy of watching me with another woman, so, perhaps, this was it. I blinked and I could feel my eyelashes brushing the velvet blindfold as I was still trying to look around at what was being done to me, even though I was in total darkness.

I didn't have time to follow this train of thought for long when a mouth closed down over a nipple and with a swirl of tongue and a strong suck, it tore me back to complete focus on every inch of my skin.

The crazy thrill of sexual sensation when you can't see who it is making you squirm is delicious and alarming and ridiculously exciting. Yes, he did say excited, didn't he?

Again, I was immediately brought out of my thoughts and into my body as a lick touched my other nipple. Just seconds later I felt another lick, this one slower and deeper within the lips of my vagina.

What a thing it is to limit senses and information not knowing how long it will be between contacts and will it be a tongue, a hand, another body part and where will it land next? Another suck on the other nipple followed by a lick to my pussy that happened so soon after, that whoever was tasting me like this, could not have gotten from one place to the other so fast! Were there two people in this room? Was one of them Benjamin? This was maddening and fantastically confusing.

Nipple and pussy were now in two different mouths. I had established that fact and was processing it. Their gentle and then firm tonguing and sucking continued until I was very wet and starting to move towards the uphill climb to orgasm. I felt a finger slide into me while the tongue continued and I let out a moan of pleasure and the nipple being sucked received a long hard pull heightening the sensation. Then nothing... just silence...no touches for almost a minute or maybe it was an hour. I'd lost sense of time trying to determine who, exactly, was administering this wet dream style of attention to my body.

Cool air. Someone or some people were blowing cool air onto the wet nipple and the wetter pussy that was still humming after being brought so close to the edge. I could feel how hard my nipples were and shook my head to try and regain some clarity when the tongue returned between my restrained legs with a steady lapping. I couldn't help but move my hips with the rhythm of what was happening to my lower body, and the second person returned to the nipple they had been tonguing with their wet mouth and together, they began again, to ramp me up to orgasm. I was exhaling trying to maintain control when I felt a mouth on my other nipple. I gasped.

Wait. Another mouth now? Three? There are three people in this room with me? Males? Females? We had just eliminated the "me with another woman" scenario and moved on to something that Benjamin obviously had a deeper need to experience. I had agreed. Anything he wanted. And he did say there would be no pain or punishment, so I worked on calming my mind that was racing wildly and felt, really felt, what was happening on my skin. He said I would be safe. I pictured the heat Benjamin was feeling as this hedonistic and other worldly scene, his fantasy scene, played out under his direction.

Hard pulls on tender places made me moan and strain against the velvet ropes, closing up my body as much as I could, and a moment later opening wider as these three strangers took sensitive parts of me into their mouths, wetting each place over and over with tongues and lips and nipping with teeth. So much! Too much! Not enough!

As my mind was reeling, I suddenly smelled Benjamin's cologne. It was nearby. I felt a mouth nuzzle at the hollow of my throat and a tongue move the garnet drop on the velvet choker I wore. Then it was him, his face near mine and I recognized our electric current and his scent as I felt his mouth cover mine, pressing me with a deep and passionate kiss. "You ... are a goddess right now." He whispered in that voice, directly into my mouth while the mouth at my pussy and the two at each breast continued their ministrations to my body. Burning fire and heat from somewhere in the center of me was pouring over every inch of my skin.

What? FOUR! Four people were here, doing this to me. I never heard a single one enter the room, yet here they were and what they were doing to my body was beyond imagination. The mouths moved away. It was quiet now. "Benjamin!" I said "What's happening?"

"Shhhhhh." Was all the answer I would get.

A breast brushed past my face and for a second the erect nipple brushed my cheek and I could smell perfume and a sugary body lotion. The soft weight of the breast pressed my cheek and I felt the nipple teasing across my now, hyper sensitive lips. A lick to my pussy happened then. A moment later, both nipples were rolled and pinched in someone's hand. The series repeated then, lips brushed, lick given, nipple pinched. He must be giving silent hand signals to whomever he has brought into this game of his because they continued now, more rapidly until my hips were grinding. My mouth was open and when the offered nipple touched my tongue, I drew it into my mouth

The motions were steady again and my body returned to climbing towards orgasm. Almost there…a pause…a long pause…I could feel my cunt muscles pulsing… and then… I felt a very familiar cock slide into me as this orchestrated playing of my body like a wind instrument continued. We all, whoever "we" included, were moving in harmony and I was calling out to the mother of god when I felt him pick up the speed and the depth of his thrusting while the tongues, in turn, worked harder at their tasks to send me over the edge.

On the edge! Over the edge! Over the god dam edge! I was crying out now and moving my body in some wild dance that bodies do when reason has disconnected from inhibition and you have become a creature, born out of flames and ancient carnal sorcery. Stars whirling beneath the velvet blindfold, heart … beat … pounding in my ears and electric … live … wire … jolts … hit me, one … after

... the ... other ... after ... the ... other and suddenly ... all touch stopped.

I was empty and it was only the soft air conditioning that touched me anywhere now and I let my body calm and sink back onto the bed. It was quiet as I listened to myself panting like I'd just run a marathon and I'm sure my face, my cunt and my breasts were flushed crimson with exertion and riotous pleasure.

A few moments later, I felt hands reaching near my face and loosening the blindfold and as he pulled it off me, Benjamin, shirtless and wearing a pair of loose cotton pants, looked down at me just like the cat that swallowed the canary. Perhaps he had.

"Holy Fuck, Benjamin! You can certainly create one hell of an elaborate fantasy." He gently undid the ropes that had bound my wrists to this hotel suite bed. I let my eyes adjust to the lighting.

Looking around the room, I noted that whoever had been here and pleasured my body while Benjamin watched his birthday fantasy come true, they were all gone now. I would never know who they were. And Benjamin would, of course, never tell me. It was one of his special fantasy scenarios where little psychological bits of it go on and on, even years later. I would always wonder if it had been anyone I knew that had played his game with me, or the lovely young woman who had tied me, or perhaps, an escort service he had hired.

It's a heady thing to fall under the powerful persuasion of another person. And it never ceased to amaze me how people with money can so easily enlist others into joining their very private games. Money is power. Sex is also power, and in this little world where I'd unwittingly become his courtesan, Benjamin was the emperor.

I sat up rubbing my wrists where they had chaffed from the tightening that happened while I was out of control. When he had freed my ankles from the restraints, he reached to a side table and produced a velvet ribbon with a small diamond heart charm dangling from it. He wrapped it on my wrist and locked the clasps that held it on. "To remind you … of tonight." He whispered. I already wore a gold anklet chain he had given me after another one of our sessions. He had said when he saw it there on my body, that it made him hard remembering how I had "earned" it. He wrapped me in his arms then and kissed me deeply saying, "Thank you. That was the best birthday present I have ever had."

He asked me to keep the red velvet bustier on because he liked it and we still had all night in the suite. I asked if anyone else would be joining us again and he said no, just he and I until we checked out in the morning. He took my hand and led me towards the parlor where he poured champagne and toasted to a fantasy fulfilled and his very, very happy birthday gift.

"You do realize, don't you" I said, "that some people are perfectly happy with a pony … and a cake?" Handing him the small box that contained the Visconti fountain pen I'd bought him as my gift, I added, "Somehow, this just sort of pales in comparison to what you just got yourself. Happy Birthday, Benjamin."

"Some mornings, it's just not worth chewing through the leather straps"

Emo Phillips

Chapter 13

Cabo San Lucas 1976

OVER

Stream of consciousness flow
<u>Game</u>

In the crowded elevator… his arm comes over my shoulder from behind … protectively … or so it seems … to anyone looking at us in the corner … they do not see his hand has stolen … beneath my coat … inside my blouse … beneath my bra … to find my nipple with his fingers … and he plays there … his secret game … pinching and twisting as I stifle gasps … hoping these strangers haven't felt my heat.

<u>Still</u>

In the pool … night swimming at my apartment … I am floating and resting my head … back on his shoulders … floating … as neighbors talk and swim 20 feet away … he is wrapping his arm around my waist now … pulling me close to sit on his lap … his hidden hand is moving my suit clear of my cunt ... and he sits me ... down ... on his hard cock ... filling me completely ... I arch ... he holds me tighter around my waist ... held there ... tight ... full of him ..."Don't move. Just sit still."... I want to move ... I want to slide him in and out but my neighbors are 20 feet away chatting ... and I sit ... still ... fine ... we can play your game ... with this small change ... pulsing cunt muscles ... kegel ... trying to squeeze him with muscles ... trying to milk him while he holds me still ... the neighbors never see me move ... but I do ... and then your game is turned on you. Let's see you try not to cum ... while I milk you with my cunt muscles ... with my neighbors 20 feet away ... in this darkened swimming pool.

Now

Cum for me ... make yourself cum while I watch ... I want to see how you hold your fingers ... how fast you move them ... how many ... how you keep them slick ... I want to watch you now ... do it.

Ride

He has me on my hands and knees now ... my hair twisted ... held in his hand ... like reins on a mare and then he slides into me ... holding my head fast ... guiding every movement with his reins ... pulling tightly on my hair as he rides ... into me ... my hips high ... head pulled back now as he brings me up ... so we are both on our knees and my head is back to his chest ... pulling tightly on my mane ... he holds me there and rides me to the stars ... until I buck ... and cry out from the pleasure/pain that races through me ... night horses.

Call

On my phone and talking to my client ... he comes to my desk chair and slides ... his hand under my skirt ... parting panties ... sliding fingers inside me ... gliding ... stroking as I ... discuss the details of the contract that will bring the job ... into my studio and pay my bills for several months ... listening ... and answering ... with uh-huhs ... and yeses ... as his fingers dance in my juice ... and whirl across my clit while I ... talk business on my phone.

Touch

In the car and driving north ..."Touch me", he says ... while he drives ... and I run my hands over his crotch until I feel the dragon waking. I'll go one better ... I move next to him and loose him ... and pull his cock into my mouth ... and listen to his breathing change ... as he accelerates ... while I move my mouth on him until he is close ... and then I let him hang ... laughing ... I slide back to my seat ... waving at the trucker who had pulled beside his car ... and caught my matinee.

You

Your arms wrapped behind me ... your hands grasping onto my shoulders ... you're plunging now into my ocean ... waves of your emotion ... crashing into you ... the shoreline of your careful distance has been found ... beaches of your private island breeched ... and now you ... your emotion ... crashing into ... your mouth ... hungry ... hungry for my mouth as you finally ... look into my eyes and see what ... I have known all along ... holding me all along ... all along my body you are touching now ... all along, what has been beside you since the start ... trying to fold me now ... hold me now ... into every space that you have realized my hands ... have been ... and soon .. will not be ... I am the secret flower who has bloomed for you at midnight for this final time ... you ... you will miss me when I'm gone.

"I'd like to meet the person who invented sex and see what they're working on now."

Author Unknown

Chapter 14

Scivu, Sardinia 1989

Can We Make You Lunch?

I played with the colors dancing on my eyes by squeezing the lids shut tighter so the light peeking through would swirl red or yellow or deep magenta under the blazing afternoon sun. I hadn't been this tan in years and certainly not over so much of my body, but the privacy and the lure of the deck made me want to feel the sun everywhere. The sun, for me, is an aphrodisiac, never having reached that almost too warm skin sensation and not fought the urge to peel off the fabric to bare what my bikini is covering and find a way to feed the cat.

Getting squirmy now, I shaded my eyes against the Sardinian sun and had a look around to see what the others were up to. Luca was lying on the deck with a rolled up towel under his head, one knee bent and a tanned foot flat on the wood surface. He was lost in the gentle rocking of the sailboat on the water, drifting in and out of slumber. God, he was a fun. His long swimmer's body; all hidden steel muscles when he was elongated like this, was deceiving in its soft look. Later, when he would bring himself up to prop on his elbow and have a look around, those now long muscles in his back and arms will coil and form rock hard ridges, defined and delineated beneath his coppery skin and when I see that happen on a body like that, I coil a muscle too, deep between my legs.

I rose up from the floor of the deck and headed towards the galley in search of something cold to drink, leaving my discarded top on my towel. In the cool shade below deck, I braced my arm on the upper cupboard while I leaned in towards the chill air of the fridge. Gina wandered in and draped her body over my back, cupping my breasts like a makeshift bra as they hung down and looked over the food in the box along with me.

"What's looks good in there?" she asked while she dropped her chin to my back, pressing the flesh of her body onto me. Luca had a crew policy that he playfully endorsed whenever there was a private place to moor, and sometimes under sail when he was feeling the salt air call to his inner pirate: no tops on deck.

"Not a big selection; some yogurt, a little fruit, a few carrots, water, some fruit juice. We really need to make a run to the market when we dock." She abandoned my breasts and started rummaging through the cupboards and listed off the finds. "Peanut butter, very little coffee, honey, a few cans of soup, some crackers. Ugh, you're right; we need a market visit before tonight. What are you hungry for?"

"No idea. I could eat something, but I think I'm hungrier for a little Luca sandwich." I teased. A giggle escaped her throat. "I know! He's so yummy. I could just eat him up." She purred and the sound rolled into a wicked chuckle.

She leaned out the door and called up to the deck. "Luca! Can we make you lunch?"

"Si! That would be great. Gina? Can you bring up water, also?" he called back down.

"Of course. We'll be right up."

I could almost see the plan formulating behind those chocolate eyes. "No!" I said. "Are you thinking what I'm thinking?'

She grabbed the plastic bottle of honey from the shelf and waggled her eyebrows at me. We dashed around the small galley, laughing, while collecting "interesting" foods by texture and thickness for our Luca lunch. I found a tray to carry our goodies and we headed back up on deck into the hot sun.

He was sitting up when we got there, shading his eyes with an arm thrown across his forehead when Gina handed him the water bottle and he twisted the cap off to take a drink. I had settled the cloth covered tray on a deck chair and lowering the bottle from the long drink he had taken, he wiped his mouth with his wrist asking what we had found.

Gina took the water bottle from his hands and gently pushed him back down on the deck and she reached for the sides of his swim trunks. She began to slide them down his long legs making him laugh and then she shared her menu plan. "We are going to make you, lunch."

Revealing the tray's contents, I selected the vanilla yogurt and with a serving spoon, I took a healthy portion and proceeded to deposit it along the length of his awakening cock. While I slipped out of my string bikini bottom, Gina had the honey bottle and she used it like a cake decorator would and wrote yummy in a thin line from his neck down to his balls while he laughed and called us gatti selvaticis.

Sliding my tongue down the shaft of his cock before the yogurt slipped off his body, he moaned and laughed at the same time that Gina caught his throat with a nip and began to lick the honey she had dribbled there. We savored our Luca lunch and when Gina arrived at my location, I added more yogurt and together we licked our way up the sides of his now rock hard cock and took turns sliding it into our mouths, stopping occasionally to swirl our yogurt and Luca coated tongues together and find our way back down towards the hot sacks below. We each pulled one into our mouths and gently rolled our tongues around it. Up we went again, twining tongues and licking the shaft while Luca undulated as he laughed and growled at our attention to our food.

On her knees beside him and bending forward to her task, his hand found the moist cave of Gina's sex and with one hand massaging her rounded ass, he dipped and plunged and strummed her pussy with the other. We brought him to a climax there in the hot day sun and with the remains of the yogurt, honey and salty taste of Luca on my face I slithered my way up his body to share the flavor with our captain.

Never one to miss an opportunity, I felt a cold dollop of yogurt on the shallow of my back and Gina's teeth as she nipped my ass on her way to her meal. She licked at the yogurt and with her tongue, she sent it on a journey between my cheeks and dancing across my bud and down to where it coated my cunt and then she followed, cleaning the cool sweet sauce as she went. Luca held me there massaging my back with long strokes from shoulder to ass as

Gina dipped her tongue inside me and sucked the yogurt from my arousal swollen lower lips.

Luca slipped out from under me and reached for a ripened peach. He took a juicy bite above me and together, he and Gina turned me onto my back. He let the juice from the peach fall down onto my body and having pulled the stone from the fruit and tossed it over board; he ran the wet flesh of the peach around my nipples and chased the juice with his tongue, leaving some for Gina. I watched these two, my summer lovers, as they feasted and nipped and licked their way across my body and I threw my head back and up to the hot sun and let the sensation wash over me like a wave. I ran my hands through their hair as they went, watching when their tongues met at the middle of my legs, now spread wide as Luca lifted my pussy to his mouth with his hands under my ass. He rubbed the peach against my cunt and lapped the juice away and Gina got the peanut butter and spread a finger full on each of my nipples and took her time licking and sucking them clean again. When peach juice was thoroughly mixed with my own juice I'd offered with my orgasm, I reached for Gina and hauled her up to my mouth and with her legs straddling me, we kissed passionately while Luca raised her to her knees above me and took her from behind.

He came again, inside her, and they collapsed forward, with me beneath them both, but I took their weight, too exhausted to complain. When it became hard to breathe, they laughed with me and rolled off my sated body.

"We need to go to town for more food, Luca." I told him as I drank the last of my Pelligrino. He agreed.

Gina looked over at us while she brushed her wild and tangled golden hair back over her shoulder saying, "That's fine you two, but tonight, dinner is on me."

I laughed out loud and getting to my feet, ran to the side and launched myself out into the air and dove down beneath the blue waters of this deep and private cove on the Costa Verde.

"You never lose by loving.
You always lose by holding back."
Barbara DeAngelis

Chapter 15

Dublin 1992

Irish Love Song

It was a Saturday night, my fifth day in Dublin photo-graphing pubs and live music performances for a trendy travel magazine. I had taken some good shots of a dozen spots where locals and tourists had wandered in for a pint and great music. I'd been to Ireland before doing the sight-seeing thing, but moving around only from mid afternoon until the wee hours of the morning was a very different perspective of this charming old city.

As night falls, the bar people begin to emerge from homes or day jobs and they slip into things that cling and grab them in all the right places so some lad or lass will re-turn the favor as the night wears on. I had already cleared permission to photograph the entertainment that night at Whelan's, a hip and lively place that's been a part of the Dublin scene for years.

The bar owner had said to arrive about ten p.m. when things really got going. I made my way up the line at the door with my gear bag slung over my shoulder and the giant door bouncer waved me forward. We'd met a few days earlier and he had given me some great tips about other places for pictures around town. He hadn't steered me wrong. I now had an amazing array of images from local favorites playing traditional Irish music to head banging Celtic devils covered in ink and metal studs emerging from unlikely places.

"Hey, Nolan!" I touched his arm as I got to the door. He leaned down so I could hear him. "Pandora, darling, how'd ya do with that list a pubs?" I had to speak up over the crowd noise even out here. "They were great! I got some good stuff. And Copper's was insane! I think I lost my virginity again just trying to squeeze through the crowd to the toilets." He laughed loud and hearty and put his arm around me as he led me safely to the stage door where I'd meet the bands. "All right then girl. Have a ged time and let me know if ya nyed anathin."

I shook hands with the backstage manager and he yelled out over the noise of tuning up, raucous chatter and scale runs of smoky voices. "Pipe down ya slagging goms! Say hallo to Pandora Bleue." Some loud cat calls carried across the room. "Shut it! She's a photographer for Urban Tribes Magazine and she'll be taking pictures of the shows tonight. She's fair play so treat her kindly and for fuck's sake, try and keep ya knickers on." I heard a cacophony of various greetings shouted my way. One randy fellow drumming his sticks on a wall asked if I wanted to immortalize any record breaking pipe, tapping a stick on the front of his pants.

"Honey," I said lifting my camera bag slightly. "This is a camera, not a microscope." The room roared with laughter. "Ouch!" "Ay, she's in!" "Gawd, I'm in love!" and half a dozen other shouts of encouragement rang out as I made my way to an arm chair to open my gear bag.

"Well done with the volley back at that fuckwit, Colin." A sassy black haired girl said, laughing, as she handed me a perfectly poured Guinness. She was one of the servers and accustomed to coming back into "the bull pen" to deal with these "wankers" as she called them. "Give me a shout if you nyed anathing, eh?" I gave her a nod and unpacked a camera and slung it over my neck.

It seemed like everywhere I turned that night there was some magical combination of spotlights and curls of smoke, beautiful faces straining over a blistering guitar or a drummer lost in the motion of the pounding beat he was making. Great stuff for the black and white spread I was shooting and the choice to leave off the color work gave it a timeless look as well.

Somewhere around midnight, the headliners took the stage and the full to capacity crowd, swaying and drunk on music and ale went wild. I had seen the other band members backstage but the lead singer must have arrived after I'd moved out to the main floor of the bar to shoot from the crowd and side stage. Colin, the fuckwit, sat at the drum kit rolling out a steady beat that held up the bottom of their song.

The singer held the microphone down with his hand like it was going to float away if he didn't and when the light hit him, he sent the first notes out across the room and they went into my ears and settled somewhere in my panties. His voice was scratchy and sexy from cigarettes and a late night life moving from shadows to spotlights. I don't get swoony like a teenager over celebrities or entertainers that I have to interact with in my line of work. It's a hazard and you start making stupid decisions that could cost you future jobs when you think with your twat.

He was standing there in that hot white light in his leather vest and black pants, bare arms with lovely strong biceps and some words inked on him that I couldn't read because of the angle. His dark hair was pulled back in a ponytail and a gold hoop, like a pirates, glistened from one ear and I just couldn't keep my eyes off him. I went through a hundred shots of the band and at least eighty were of him. He was rough and tousled and beautiful up there. You could feel the way the audience reacted to him; every woman wanted him and every man wanted to be him. Eoghan lit up the night and the crowd would have started a riot for him if he'd asked.

I was getting too warm in my leather jacket for several reasons and I peeled if off, clearing my camera strap as I did. Nolan, just a few feet away, saw me and waved for me to toss the coat and he made a key locking gesture telling me he would put it back in the office for safe keeping. I nodded and sent it sailing into his waiting hands.

Moving to the music when I raised my camera to my eye, I turned back to the stage and was startled to see Eoghan's face in the telephoto lens, staring straight at me and reaching my way with an open hand as he sang and held eye contact. I was sure it was the camera he was playing to with the dead sexy look and the come-on hand motion. I smiled and kept shooting, making sure that whoever saw these shots would imagine it was them he was choosing in this sea of flesh and that he had big plans for them after the show. Sexy shots sell no matter what the subject matter is. People want to look right into the eyes of the object of their desire and they want to see that desire reflected back. It was electrifying.

The show ended and the crowd wandered out. The bar crew began their closing duties. I took some shots of this more solemn and oddly beautiful ritual that happens in every music venue worldwide after the shows are over. I was sitting on a bar stool taking some photos of Colleen, who had brought me the beer early on, as she leaned on the bar talking with Nolan.

"Did you get some interesting pictures?" the smoky voice said from just behind me. I turned and Eoghan was standing with his hands in his front pockets like a kid waiting to ask his mother if he could go out to play.

"Yes, I did! That last set and the way you looked into the camera was very hot. They'll look great in the magazine spread. I'm sure of it."

"I wasn't lookin at the camera, darlin'. I was lookin at you." he said and a gorgeous smile crept across his face.

"Oh… my…" I looked down embarrassed as I tried hard to rein in my grin. "That's very flattering. The show was terrific, the way you and your band perform together; it feels like you've known each other forever."

"Yeah. We have since we were lads. Pandora, wasn't it?"

"Oh, yes. I'm sorry. I didn't mean to be rude. Pandora Bleue. Please, call me Pan." I offered my hand and he held it a bit too long.

"Well, Pan, it's a pleasure to meet you. I'm Eoghan Foley."

"Eoghan. Oh, it's pronounced like I-A-N? I saw the posters but wasn't sure I had it right."

"It's an ancient spelling, but you're right. It's pronounced like Ian. And how did you come by a name as interesting as Pandora Bleue?"

"Ah, the name, well, it's a French surname and I had a mother who was very interested in mythology."

"Ahh. I'll bet you're full of road warrior stories. Would ya like to go grab some food and talk a bit?"

"Um, actually, that sounds just about perfect. I haven't eaten anything since…um… lunch… yesterday? Wow, I didn't realize it had been that long. I'm starving. Let me get my things gathered and my coat and I'll meet you in a minute." He smiled again.

"We can't have you starvin' in my country, now can we?"

I collected my gear while Nolan fetched my jacket for me. With hugs all around, I made my farewells to the bar folk with a promise to them that I would send prints from the shoot for their walls. Eoghan was waiting just inside the front door and when I turned back for a final wave, Colleen gave me the double thumbs up sign and she rocked her body like she was humping her man. I was laughing, and sure my cheeks were flushed, as he held the door open for me and we made our way out to the Dublin street. "They're good people. Just tightly wound by the end of the night," he offered.

We caught a taxi to the quietest of the only four all night restaurants in the city. We shared plates of food and cups of tea and talked about everything we could think of until the sun was coming up. He had asked what was next on my itinerary for Ireland and I told him I'd booked a rental car and a small cottage over in Galway County just to get away for a few days. He was also free for the week, with his next gig in Glasgow, Scotland on the following Saturday.

He asked if he could crash my private party and come along with me on my road trip as he was in dire need of air that wasn't filled with exhaust fumes. I was thrilled that he'd want to spend more time together as I felt we still had so much more to say. When the cab dropped me back at my hotel to change and pack, he gave me his address and drew a map to his place in Rathmines where I would pick him up about two that afternoon.

In my room, I grabbed a shower and packed my things back into my one travel bag and called the front desk for a noon wakeup call and then I stretched out on the bed for a short sleep to recharge my exhausted body. It felt like my eyes had been closed for fifteen minutes when the phone rang, but checking my watch it was noon already. I made a pot of tea with the small carafe in the room and spent some time organizing my notes and equipment and then I set out to try and make my hair and face look presentable for this Emerald Isle road trip.

By two, I had pulled the Audi up outside Eoghan's flat and he sauntered out showered and shaved and dressed in a crisp white t-shirt, jeans and a leather jacket that looked eerily similar to mine. He tossed his bags in the boot and as he got into the car, I laughed as I realized we were wearing the exact same thing and we even had our dark hair pulled back in a tail down our backs and similar versions of aviator sunglasses. "If you're wearing the same bra and thong that I have on, I am going to be seriously disturbed mister." He laughed loudly and said, "Great minds woman…great minds."

The first half of the drive was an easy ride west with pleasant countryside along the roadways. We talked non-stop and he turned the stations of the radio to see what the locals were listening to then he'd sing along with some of the songs and I joined in when I knew the lyrics. "You've a lovely voice Pan. Have you ever thought of singing on a stage?"

"Not a chance in hell. I'd be sick as a dog with nerves."

"Truly? Now here I thought you'd be afraid of nothing."

He went back to a story he was telling about his trip to the states and when he saw the sign for Athlone just ahead he asked me to make a stop there so he could clear something up. I took that as guy code for needing a pee.

I made my way off the M6 and we found a tea shop in town. Parking the car in the lot, I got out stretching my legs. Eoghan came around the car and slid his hands under my jacket and pulled me towards him and into a first kiss so sweet that it made my knees buckle. He moved back a bit so we could look at each other from inches away. "I've been waiting since just after midnight to do that and I couldn't wait any longer."

He kissed me again and I felt some sort of locked door click, tumble and fall open someplace deep inside of me. I didn't say it out loud, but this, right here, was what I fear the most. Sex is, in the end, a fancy handshake. But when you give away a piece of light from your heart, it means something real and it's a piece of you that you'll never get back again.

We stopped in the tea shop and bought some take away cups and a few small snacks and I tossed him the keys to take us into Galway County. We made our way to Doonreagan and the seaside cottage I'd reserved and found the key under the flower pot, right where the rental agent said it would be. The kitchen was stocked as I'd request-ed and there were bottles of wine and ale and fresh fruit and flowers on the side board and table. "This is gorgeous! Look at all this! We could stay here for days and never need anything from the outside world!"

I took a tour around the little house and saw that it had all the amenities and water views from all the back windows. Eoghan had put our bags in the same bedroom, so it looked like we were doing this, sex and all. I was ready but I could feel a pull in my heart like a small rip was beginning.

"Are you thirsty, Eoghan? I could make tea or there's wine or maybe I can find something else in here..." I called from where I was bending over inspecting the con-tents of the refrigerator.

"Nope; not thirsty right now, thank you."

"OK. Are you hungry? I could cook something or make a sandwich?"

"Nope. Not hungry, not for food, anyway."

I looked around the open door as he came towards me.

He took my hand and led me back to what was to be our room and sitting on the edge of the bed, he pulled me to him so I was standing between his legs. He pulled my face down to him and kissed me the way he had in the parking lot the first time. He kissed my lips, my eyes, my cheeks and my neck in a slow and tender way.

"I think it's time to see if we're wearing matching un-derwear as well," I joked. I peeled off my leather jacket and he stood and did the same. When I went to reach for my shirt, he stopped my hands and reached just under it, touching my skin for the first time and slid it slowly up and over my head. He let me take his shirt off and we stood for a moment like we had a thousand years ahead to draw out these first touches.

He held me and we moved like we were slow dancing. We moved our hands wherever there was no clothing. It was innocent and sensual and dare I say it, loving. I pulled the tie out of his hair and let it fall down and he took mine away and ran his fingers through and fanned my hair out over my shoulders.

He loosened my jeans and we pulled off our boots. I loosened his jeans and we let them both drop to the floor where we kicked them aside and returned to our embrace with more skin to touch and revel in. It was slow, the way we moved, like an opium dream, with hands as soft as velvet. As the layers of clothing came away, one and then another, we stopped each time and brushed our hands over what had been revealed, sealing each newly charted place with kisses. When finally, we were both free of all our clothing and we had smoothed our hands over each other in the lightest, gentlest way that lovers can, he moved me back to the bed and I laid down for him.

I looked deep into his clear blue eyes. "Oh man, you're gonna break my heart Eoghan Foley... and I am gonna to let you."

Every touch, this first time, was soft as a whisper. He kissed my lips and cupped my breast and kissed each nipple as if I could break any second like a china teacup under too much pressure. What a far cry this experience was from the other lovers I have taken to my bed that had pounced and twisted and howled at the moon. This was something different and this bed, on this day, was sacred space.

The soft beauty of this touching had me entranced as he slipped inside of me that first time. I felt tears falling while he made real, honest, love to me. I was no virgin but I felt like one in his arms that day. The rhythm of his movement and the way he never broke eye contact and never stopped bringing his lips to mine was far more intimate than any wild fucking I have ever experienced.

That steady burn built between us and with tears on my face and a loud cry from me, he moaned with a sound like a broken angel and we came together that first time, Eoghan and I.

We had only four days at that cottage before our lives would send us off in two different directions. We walked the beach and shopped in the village where he bought me an Aran sweater and insisted I should always wear it braless so I could feel him playing with my nipples as the rough pattern teased them. We cooked in the kitchen and I photographed the country side and the ocean and him, my beautiful Eoghan, in a thousand types of light.

We made love as many times a day as we could, each time hotter and freer as the days went by, on every surface in the house, out on the beach during morning walks and under the stars on the grass in the yard.

Our physical need for each other ramped up each day until that last night when we were so wracked with grief knowing, whatever this was that we had now, our future lives would never happen in the same city, that we were savage and wild with each other. We grabbed and squeezed, plunged and sucked and we would have taken bites out of each other just to bring a little more of the other into us.

A few times in your life or perhaps only once, you know for certain, that if fate took you right that moment that you would die completely fulfilled, completely happy, because you had everything that you would ever need. For me, I knew that a moment like that had arrived, and Eoghan felt it too.

Somewhere in the middle of that last night we were exhausted from trying to fit a lifetime into a few waning hours. The linen sheets had been long since shoved off the bed and we lay there and cried into each other's hair with our bodies wrapped so tightly together that we could have been one person, one breath, one heartbeat.

We were quiet on the drive back to Galway where I had a red eye flight bound for Los Angeles to catch. He held my hand on his lap as he drove. We couldn't speak around the lumps in our throats so I took his arm and kissed the tattoo there that said the last line from the Leonard Cohen anthem, "There's a crack in everything. That's how the light gets in."

The farewell with my beautiful Irish lover squeezed my heart hard and I dragged my bags up the jet way to my plane. As we lifted off and the lights on the dark coastline fell away from my window view, I was wrapped in the sweater and the sweet sadness of the hardest thing we ever do; to let go and walk on when it's what needs to happen next. I could feel the place in my heart where my piece of light had always lived; feeling the hole that would remain from where I'd given that part to Eoghan.

"Love's mysteries in souls do grow, but yet the body is his book."

John Donne

Chapter 16

Miami 1993

Finding Venus

It was my turn to host our pot luck bitch festival and the girls and I were opening our second bottle of wine. The Four Bushketeers have been friends for more than fifteen years and our devoted little circle is the singular constant that gets us through our lives. We gather for regular Cock-Tales & Whine or when one of us hits a rough patch and needs the kind of support that can only be found with the women who know you best.

Robin is married now with two darling children. She adores her husband, but occasionally, things settle into a dull routine and the rest of us jump to her aide with sizzling advice. She puts it to good use back at home and that always slaps a stupid smile on her husband's face for awhile, so he encourages the bitch fest, knowing his Robin will come home with a brand new trick up her sleeve for his pleasure.

Diane, my nearest and dearest, was married in her 20's and has no interest in a repeat performance as she has far too much fun sampling from the smorgasbord of men that gravitate to her anytime she enters the room. I introduced her to one of my fuck buddies, Oliver, and they have their own play dates on occasion and it's given us many an evening's entertainment as we share and compare Ollie stories while Robin shrieks with nervous laughter and Shawna prods us for more details.

Shawna was the one we had gathered for that night. Her cheating dog of a husband had finally left her for a junior attorney at his law firm. She was as much relieved that the lying was over as she was destroyed that she'd given him twelve years and a dozen chances to stop his wandering and in the end he'd left anyway. We wanted to be there for her and help her through this transition and into a new life, minus the scumbag.

After she had given us the details and vented a bit about it, she hadn't wanted to dwell much longer on the topic and deftly turned our talk towards other subjects.

I'd made my famous lobster risotto and as I carried in to the table, I called for someone to turn on some music and grab the salad on the sideboard. Robin cranked on the radio and over the airwaves, there was Eoghan's band playing a song I had heard them perform a year earlier in Dublin.

Diane caught my head droop and the slow inhale as I set the serving dish down and let the music wash over me for the moment. I was several months into a self imposed break from sex while I spent this time focusing on work and undoing the knots in my heart from the almost everything love affair and our sad parting. "You OK?" she queried, laying a hand on my arm. "Yep." I said resolutely. "Fine. It just took me by surprise."

She got up and found some other music for us to listen to and returning to the table, now laden with food, she clapped her hands together loudly like a kindergarten teacher. "All right, Bitches! Enough of this shit! Shawna needs to shake the douche bag out of her life. Robin needs a break from the kids and the husband. Pan's still got the Irish lover boy's songs burning in her loins and I just need to get the hell out of L.A. for a few days. We are going to Miami. We are staying in my condo. We are going shopping. We are having a spa day, and we are leaving all the cock and bullshit behind. No guy talk. No sex talk. Who's in?" Four hands went up. "That's my girls!" she said triumphantly.

The following weekend, we were lounging on pool chairs at Diane's South Beach condo and working our way through a pitcher of margaritas. I'm not sure why we ever imagined the four of us could actually drink margarita's and not eventually be laughing ourselves sick over something involving sex.

Not surprisingly, Diane was the first to break the rules. We had just seen a "raisin", as the elderly sun worshippers in SoBe are called. She had sauntered past us wearing a questionable choice of a leopard bikini, and Diane was gripped with an uncontrollable case of the giggles. Shawna elbowed her, "You're so bad! She might hear you!" Diane shook her head suppressing another giggle. "No! It's not her." Off she went again starting with small chuckles, a twitter and a squeak. She calmed down and the next one would hit her and off she would go again until we were all doing it. Like yawning, giggling is infectious, so when I caught my breath, I threw a hand full of ice at her. "OK. Give it up. What's so damn funny?"

"Ollie" she gasped and giggled again.

"Ollie? You're giggling over an Ollie sex story aren't you? Weren't you the one who proclaimed this a sex free weekend? Give it up, Wexler." Between fits and giggles she told us that after a particularly "vigorous" session of fun fucking, that Ollie had stood up on the bed and let out an impressive Tarzan yell. That had us screaming with laughter.

A few minutes later Robin, between giggles added a story. "One time," (Laughter interruption) "when we were in high school, my parents were out and Ray came over for a quickie. So we were in the shower and my mother came into the bathroom to get something and Ray jumped up and splayed his hands and feet on the shower wall and held himself up there" (Giggling and pantomiming) "like Spiderman, so she wouldn't see him under the shower door." That had us howling.

We lazed away the afternoon sunning, reading magazines and adding more hilarious confessions to our Sex Comedy Hall of Fame; a fictitious award ceremony we had invented. Favorite Category: **Dumbest Thing A Guy Has Said To You While You Had Their Dick In Your Mouth**, the winner- "This is so much better than the can of Crisco I used yesterday." New category: **Best Quaff Story**, that embarrassingly gas-like sound that happens after Olympic fucking when your vagina has finally relaxed and releases the thirty cubic feet of air his cock has pumped into it. We were glad no one else was at the pool as we would have been ejected had they been listening.

We had a reservation at four with the spa down Ocean Avenue, so we wandered back to the condo to gather our things before leaving to walk the five block trip. Diane reserved a room where all four of us could have our massages at the same time and continue our chatting. The masseuses had an earful and at some comment or other, one had broken her serene professionalism and laughed out loud with us. Half the fun of this group is that we tend to inspire playfulness even in settings where decorum was expected.

After our muscles were pummeled into loose noodle condition, we headed to the sauna that was thankfully empty but for us. Lying on benches or leaning on walls, we were quietly sucking in steam and letting the sweat drip from our noses without even trying to stop it.

"I'm not so sure that I actually like men." Shawna's comment had us all turn our heads her way and stare, waiting for her to elaborate on her revelation. "Seriously. All that time with Dan, I feel like I had to psyche myself up to be enthusiastic in bed. I'm sure he must have felt that I wasn't 100% into his "lovemaking" … and I use that term loosely. Even the guys I was with before him, I never felt like I was really, really into it. It's like there was something really important, just … I don't know … missing."

"Like breasts and a vagina?" (Diane … always so helpful.)

We laughed and Shawna threw her hands out and said. "Yeah. I think so." That surprised us. "Every time I'd try and fantasize something to occupy my mind while Dan was pounding away, it was always, vaguely, about women. Jeesuz. Even trying to watch porn! I see these guys hung like racehorses and it just doesn't do it for me because I'm secretly watching the woman. He's ramming his two by four into her back door and I'm thinking, hello! There's a lonely clitoris waiting for some attention, right there, buddy!"

We were all laughing with her. The sun, the margaritas, the massage and the sauna had loosened her up enough to drop some long hidden truth on our circle. "So Shawna... honey... why don't you explore this? Go have a hot fling with some babe and see if your boat floats." I offered.

'Ahhhh!! I'm freaked out by the thought of virgin girl sex. I'd so much rather have some experience before I try it for real in a bar or wherever it is you can actually meet women."

"You've been with women. You should fuck her, Pan."(Diane ... helping again.)

"What?" I shrieked "Like riding lessons? I just don't do that, you lunatic." I shot Di a look of disbelief that had us all laughing again.

It was quiet for a few minutes until I said, "Although...I do know how we could get you some experience from a trustworthy source...if you're game."

A while back, I had written an article with a photo spread on the personal stories of escorts, strippers and call girls in Miami. I spent a week taking notes and photos at the strip clubs and interviewing the entertainers that offered "full service" to high end clients. I was introduced to an interesting, and surprisingly sweet sex worker. I later assisted her in securing a very lucrative endorsement contract and she promised to return a favor anytime. Sandy wasn't one of the angry pretend lesbians that show up in porn movies slapping, finger ramming and scowling their way through scenes that some sleazy male film maker had dreamed up. She was a soft, passionate bisexual woman, who had managed to maintain a sense of mental balance and wonderful femininity even in that hardcore world.

I told Shawna about Sandy and she agreed that this would be the perfect way for her to safely explore her curiosity. I made the call and set up the "date" for later that evening. As we walked back from the spa to the condo, Shawna was a bundle of energy.

Back at Diane's, we had ordered some food for delivery but Shawna was too nervous to eat anything. Sandy would be there at nine and, in a brave move, Shawna asked us to stay at the condo and be there if she needed us for morale support.

We all decided to dress her up in something that made her feel sexy. Shawna and Diane were roughly the same build, so Diane dragged us into her walk in closet to find some "funderwear" for Shawna from a collection so extensive that it made mine look sad, and I love my lingerie. Robin was pawing through the silks and garters and she pulled out a one piece, black fishnet, crotch less body suit that she held up exclaiming, "Oh…My…God! This is SO hot!"

I was over at one of the dressers sorting through the tamer items and found a pretty floral patterned corset. Shawna already had a pair of panties on that almost matched, so I handed it to her saying, "This is it. It's sweet and it's sexy and the hug around your ribcage will make you courageous for this inaugural landing on the Pussy Planet."

"Thanks, Pan." She was smiling as she took it and we made her try it on and it suited her perfectly. She turned towards me and asked, "Do you like all this girly underwear?

I mean, I've seen you dressed to kill for parties, but most of the time you're wearing your usual uniform."

"My uniform? Huh?" I was confused.

"Oh, for God's sake, Pan. You are forever in a cotton t-shirt and a pair of jeans. You modify the look with long sleeves or short and heeled boots or shoes, but outside of a party, that's it babe. It's a uniform. Deal with it." (Diane … clarifying the statement)

I glanced down at my short sleeve black cotton t-shirt and my black jeans. Busted. "Fine. But this…" I unzipped my jeans and stepped out of them and ripped my t-shirt over my head to reveal my red and black lace g-string and a sassy matching bra that framed my curves nicely. I threw my hands up like a fountain, wrists together above my head and jutted my hip out. "…is where the party keeps on going."

"Oo Lala! Do you wear stuff like that all the time? I'm in granny panties over here." Robin seemed impressed and also distressed.

"Yes. I do wear things like this most every day. It's not about being prepared for ninja sex; it's about the way they make me feel about my body. I just carry myself differently and I feel sexier even if no one ever sees this but me."

After we primped and powdered and dolled Shawna up for her "date" with Sandy, we settled out on the deck with a glass of wine.

"Fuck. I feel like I'm waiting for a blind date to the prom." Shawna said.

At the knock on the door, I got up to go meet Sandy and introduce her to the girls and to Shawna who was nervous, but excited. Sandy gave me a hug and shook hands with the girls and when I brought her to Shawna, she took both of her hands and told her to relax and that it would be gentle and safe and fun. Sandy privately asked Shawna if she wanted anyone else in the room with them so she might be more comfortable.

Shawna called me aside. "Look Pan, I know this is sort of weird. OK. Very weird, but I think I'd feel more comfortable if you were in the room too. I feel like you could give me some reality checks when it's over and hell, you're a photographer. You've seen it all. Jeez!" She was on a nervous roll "… you've done it all, so it won't be a big freaking deal like it would be for Robin … and I'm afraid Diane would bring in score cards and play the Russian Gymnastics judge and I… well…"

I hugged her tight and whispered in her ear. "I'll be your spotter. I'll stay with you as long as you need me and I won't judge. I promise." I brought her hands to my mouth and kissed them. "You'll be fine. I know it."

We rejoined Sandy who was talking quietly to the others and Shawna told her I would be her safe buddy.

As we headed to Shawna's room where we had lit candles and had soft music on, she looked back at Diane and Robin and raised both her eyebrows in mock terror and they waved her on and wandered out on the deck to enjoy the beach view at night.

I folded into a chair in a corner of the room outside the candle light; away from the bed but close enough that if Shawna needed me, I would be right there.

"Sweetie, I want you to just relax and I'm going to just rub your shoulders a little so you can feel my hands on you in a non threatening or sexual way first. OK?" She had nodded and Sandy sat behind her and began to caress her shoulders and neck until Shawna started to melt into the movement of her hands.

Sandy caressed her face and ran her hands through her hair and down her arms letting Shawna feel the softness of her touch. When she felt that Shawna was ready, she put her hands on either side of her face and pulled her in for a gentle kiss and moved back a bit to see her reaction. Shawna was smiling and she leaned forward to greet her mouth again and this time, the kiss was deeper and more passionate.

Shawna reached for Sandy and they embraced and Sandy ran her hands gently over Shawna's back and down along her sides while kissing passionately and probing now with tongues, moving soft kisses down each other's necks.

"Are you ok, Sweetie? Is this all right for you?" Sandy asked her.

"Yes it's nice!" I heard the excitement in her voice.

"Now, we can do this a couple of ways. I can just let you explore me or, if you prefer, I can show you ways that you make love to a woman and you can just lay back and enjoy and then you can explore me if you'd like. Which would you prefer? There's no right or wrong here and I want this first experience for you to be perfect."

"I'm not sure what to do so, if it's ok, I'll let you show me."

I was touched at how concerned Sandy was and wondered if she was like this with all her clients. I hadn't observed her working though she had offered that I could have while I gathered my research for my article.

"Let's ease you out of some clothes first" Sandy unbuttoned the blouse Shawna was wearing and peeled it away from her body. "Oh, Shawna! I love this corset! It's very sexy." She ran her hands over it and skimmed the top edge with her pink polished nails. She had Shawna stand as she slowly peeled off her pants. "Lovely." Sandy purred as she ran her hands over Shawna's rear end and gently cupped the firmness of her cheeks. "You're a beautiful woman, Shawna." She slipped her hands between Shawna's legs and used a flat hand to rub the front of her panties making Shawna flush with color. She slowly peeled the panties off and returned to embracing her and smoothing her hands over arms, legs and round ass cheeks squeezing gently as she went. Shawna was lifting her feet and flexing her leg muscles in response to the stroking and Sandy had her lay back onto the bed.

"Now sweetheart, here comes the more interesting part of this experiment. Are you ready?" Shawna nod-ded. Sandy loosened the corset and removed it exposing Shawna's tanned and smooth body. She ran her hands sensually down the length of her body and up again. She cupped her breast and massaged it gently. "You know from experience with lovers and from touching yourself, how it feels when your breasts are touched like this. Women are going to be as diverse as male lovers. Some will want gentle touch like this. Some will want it a bit firmer like this. And some will want to really feel the connection when they pinch your nipples like this." She pinched the small points and Shawna pulled in a quick breath.

"They may want you to give their nipples a soft lick like this. Or more of a tongue massage like this." She flat-tened her tongue and circled the nipple. "Or they may want the harder contact again through sucking, like this." She starting with some rhythmic gentle sucks and then moved to a few harder ones. Shawna's legs were moving with the sudden engagement of the pussy/clit connection. From where I sat, I could see that she was already wet. Shawna seemed very comfortable with this new expression of her sexuality.

Sandy moved down between Shawna's legs now. "I'm going to begin slowly and I'd like you to watch what I'm doing here so try and sit up a bit." She did. "First, as you already know, our thighs are very sensitive." She licked a line up her inner thigh. "Sometimes, guys go straight for the pussy and mash their faces in and lick in all the wrong places to make us cum. Right?"

"Too right." Shawna agreed. Sandy continued to lick gently and trace with fingernails up and down Shawna's thighs.

"What you're going to want to do to really please a woman is to take your time. Go slow when you start and work towards the clitoris. The sensitivity builds and she'll be far more ready for a climax. Men who dive straight for your clit and then assault it with some random rhythm don't understand that it can take a really long time for you to climax that way. You'd think they would given the instructions they give us when we're returning the favor. Some men get bored with it, you know? We like a steady build up sexual tension and once our hips start moving, that should be the signal that whatever we're doing, we should keep doing it the same way until you cum, not change it up and make you go all the way back to square one again. Is it all right if I make you cum now?"

"Yes." She was breathing heavier now.

Sandy moved her hands up to the freshly waxed vulva and using her thumb and forefinger, she pushed open the hood revealing the button of her clitoris and she licked softly on either side of that sensitive place. Shawna was plenty wet now and Sandy slid a finger and then another in to her while she continued to run her tongue along the labia, while gliding her fingers in and out slowly. When Shawna's hips were rocking in a steady motion, she placed her mouth over the clitoris then and with a combination of sucks directly on the button and swirls of her tongue, Shawna cried out as she brought her to orgasm easily.

She fell back down and grabbing her own hair exclaimed that that was the best orgasm she had ever had. Sandy laughed softly and said it should always be like that and she crawled up to cradle her in her arms and kissed her gently. She let Shawna rest there on her for a moment.

Sandy asked if she wanted to know about other ways women have sex together; rough or gentle and whether she thought she was ready to give something else a try. Shawna's enthusiastic response and eagerness to learn more from Sandy was my cue to let her do the rest in private.

I got up then and smiling at them both, patted Shawna's leg. "You're in good hands here. Welcome to the new world, Babe." I left.

"Ladies, we have lift off." Diane and Robin clinked glasses with mine. I settled into the empty deck chair to look for planets and shooting stars over the Miami horizon, while our friend, who had lived a wrapped tight and compromised life for so long, found Venus in the other room.

"Tell him I'm too fucking busy – or vice versa."

Dorothy Parker

Chapter 17

San Diego 1972

Fire Starter

I've written the story about my first time having sex with a lover, it's only fair that I write the story of the first time I loved myself. Like knowing where you were the day some historical event occurred, everybody knows where, and when and how they had their first solo orgasm.

The first time I lit my own fire, and I mean touch until orgasm, I was alone in a bathtub with a massage shower head. Just weeks earlier, I'd had first time intercourse with a high school bad boy I was in serious lust with. The sensations on my body that day were ones I was anxious to recreate. I probably had that backwards. Most people discover masturbation to orgasm and then they go out and have sex. Not me. I did the deed with Aidan and weeks later discovered solo flying orgasm, alone in an empty house and thinking about him.

While at the store earlier that week, I'd bought myself a bottle of Old Spice and wore it occasionally when I wanted a little Aidan time. I was in the upstairs bathroom; a nice open space with a skylight over the main sink area. After showering and shaving wherever I could shave, I shampooed and conditioned my hair.

As I was rinsing the last of the silky conditioner from my hair, I realized I was holding a massager wand right there in my hot little hands. Idea: what if I put this between my legs and aim the water right at my pussy?

That would have meant spraying the shower head up and possibly getting the entire bathroom soaked with the overspray, so I came up with a different plan. I slid down in the tub, propping my legs apart on the tub edges and went at it again from another angle.

At first, there was a tightening and small pulsing sensation in my pussy and my propped up legs. In a few moments, I started to experience sudden jolts in my body. I was actually a little scared that I was doing something wrong that could hurt me as the jolts started happening closer together.

Some instinct told me, and maybe it was Aphrodite whispering to me, "Fuck it. People have been doing all kinds of things like this and survived. Just go for it and see what happens."

I changed the setting on the shower head to pulse and put it back between my legs. The sensation changed to a building wave and as it grew stronger, I had to force my hand to hold the shower wand still where it was and a gigantic wave of orgasm hit me.

I was staring up at the sky through the skylight and the world was moving through my 17 year old body like a freight train. It's a damn good thing I was home alone as I screamed "Holy Fuck!" at the top of my lungs. I fell back letting go of the shower head and soaking the bathroom floor to ceiling anyway.

I've moved on from shower massagers, and first lovers and have found a world filled with wondrous people and toys made for lighting your own fire, flying solo or as a Brit friend calls it, "jilling off". I say, take your pleasure into your own hands and you'll always be satisfied.

I learned quite a bit from that first solo flight as a teen. I learned that my body could go over the moon and return again and that sky lit bathrooms and the smell of Old Spice will, for all my life, give me a girl hard on.

"Remember, if you smoke after sex you're doing it too fast."

Woody Allen

Chapter 18

Laguna Beach 1980

Arresting Development

Working in my dark room, I can easily lose track of time when I find myself absorbed in a project. It's like Las Vegas in my head; no clocks anywhere in sight, no windows so you can see what time of day it is, just the laser focus of whatever my attention has locked onto. I jumped when the door buzzer rang over the speaker I had installed in the workspace at the back of my house.

I would have ignored it if I'd gone dark in here working with light sensitive film, but since I was into sorting and selection, I set my loupe aside. Making a mental note to turn the volume down on the buzzer, I got up to go and answer the door.

I could see the officer standing at the door through the frosted glass panel, unless it was some sort of repair man that had a gun holster at his waist. He saw me moving towards him. "Miss? Please open the door. I'm with the Laguna Beach Police and I need to ask you a few questions."

I unlocked the door and the officer stepped into the front hallway and closed the door behind him. "I need you to come with me, please." He took my hand and turned me around, placing the cuffs on me with my hands securely behind my back. He placed a hand on my shoulder to lead me toward the back of the house.

"Can I ask what this is about, Officer?" A moment later, we were entering my bathroom and he stopped for a second to un-cuff one hand and lifted me back to the shower area where he brought the hand back up and cuffed them both over the shower curtain bar.

Without hesitation, he reached for my jean shorts and unbuttoning them, pulled down swiftly removing them along with my panties in one motion. He reached under my t-shirt and pulled the front of it up, taking the neck hole with it until it cleared my head and sat on my shoulders like a short shrug top. He unclipped the front of my flowered bra exposing my breasts as I pressed him with questions.

"Officer! This is highly inappropriate. What's going on here? "

He ignored my question and freed his cock from his pants and turning my ass towards him, he put his foot between mine. Kicking them apart and he pushed into me and proceeded to thrust vigorously while holding my hips tightly in place. His urgency and the suddenness of the situation had me hotter than I thought I should be and pretty quickly I was arching my back and involuntarily pulling on my cuffed hands. He thrust faster now and when he came, I pulled, and the shower curtain bar came crashing down. I found myself bent over, hands to the ground along with the broken bar and my ass in the air with him still buried in me to his hips.

And then I started to laugh, hard, which has some very interesting affects on your pussy when a cock is slippery wet and still inside you. He started laughing too and circling his arms around my waist, he hauled me back up to uncuff me.

"Oliver, did you take that uniform from a props department?"

"Hell ya! I told the crew I had to go arrest a hot chick at lunch time and they waved me through the gate, easy. I'm doing stunts for a cop show this week."

"You are ridiculous; you know that, don't you?' I scolded. "What if I'd had a house full of nuns over here right now? Did you take that into account?" I was teasing him as I gathered my wits and my shorts and hopped back into my clothing.

"Well, they'd just have to wait their turn since I only have one pair of cuffs with this costume. Hey look, I had the uniform on, had a 30 minute lunch break at a location a few minutes from here and while I was playing with these cuffs in between scenes, I thought of you and your transcendental ass so, hey, carpe diem!"

"Wow, Ollie, that's so ... romantic." Laughing as I reached up to slap the front bill of his uniform hat, I added in a whisper, "Actually, it was kinda hot."

"Although," I warned, complete with accusing finger, "the whole assault and rape thing is not my cup of sex tea. It was hot because I knew you. Anyone else would have ended up with a chopstick in their eye, and thanks for teaching me that one, by the way. That said, the way you stayed in character and your dedication to your story line was excellent. Overall, I'd say it was an arresting performance."

"Thank you. And I'd like to thank the Academy and of course, my gorgeous co-star, Ms. Pandora Bleue. Without her cooperation I would have been alone in my trailer with a storyline in my head and a busy right hand."

I dragged him towards the kitchen and grabbing some things, made a quick turkey sandwich, put it in a bag with an apple and pretzels and handing it to him, shoved him back to the front door where this all started.

"Hey, I'm done about 9 tonight. I can teach you some more self-defense moves. Come on. What do ya say? Movie? Pizza? Handcuffs?" He said as he jiggled the cuffs in the air.

"Fine, but you're coming back here first and fixing my broken curtain rod, mister."

"Absolutely Miss. I'm here to serve and protect. "

With a crisp salute, he walked back out to his car and I turned, a grin crossing my face as I shook my head and headed back to the work I had left on my desk.

"Sex is one of the nine reasons for reincarnation. The other eight are unimportant."

Henry Miller

Chapter 19

Santa Monica 1997

Staring Into the Fire

I met up with my friend Claudine, over at The Galley in Santa Monica. Her call was ripe with a nervous energy as she told me she needed some clarity and lots of cocktails, stat.

After hellos and ordering drinks and appetizers, she put both hands on the table, looked at me and announced that she and Jack, her husband of seven years, wanted to experience a threesome with another woman.

"Wow. That's big. Have you guys thought this through?"

"Herein lies the problem: neither one of us have done this before so we don't really know what we're supposed to think through. Right now it just sounds different and sexy and hot. Before I jump off the high dive, I'd like to know a bit more about how deep the water is so I thought I'd enlist the wisdom of Pan on this."

"Ah, yes, of course. Considering my PhD in Relationship Psychology and Human Sexuality, I would be the obvious choice for this consultation." I was laughing into my water glass as the waiter brought our drinks and appetizers to the table.

"You know what I mean. You're just… experienced and you're, obviously, not shy about discussing things like this."

Feigning shock, I quipped, "So, you're calling me an audacious ho?"

"Pan! NO! Gawd, no, never! And in truth, if we compared score cards, mine is probably a much higher number than yours, girlfriend. It's just that the people on mine all had three legs and not two. Look, I'm nervous about what happens to me and Jack if we do this."

I put my hand over hers and patted it. "I know what you mean. I'm just giving you shit because it's fun to watch you get all flustered. "

"Bitch." She tossed her olive at me from her martini and we both laughed.

"Ok, so, you're already doing the one thing most people don't do when they consider an alternative sexual experience; you're thinking it through before you do it. Most couples get swept into the sexy tornado of imagination. All those body parts in one bed; penises, breasts, multiple vaginas and three mouths! Hell, it's an x rated Lego set and you can lose yourselves creating endless combinations of how to put the pieces together. "

She was sitting back in the red Naugahyde booth seat and listening intently now.

"Claud, the thing is that along with the extra breasts and vagina, there's a real live person who may have a messy life and maybe, a messy mind and they're bringing them along with their tube of lube. They're kind of a package deal; unless the plan is for this woman to be unconscious the whole time. If that's the case we should probably turn this chat over to a real shrink." I laughed and took a bite from the crab cake in front of me before I continued. "Look, you're going to have to talk to her before and, more importantly, you'll need to talk to her after you've mastered the three tongued crotch dive, pike position with a half twist."

"Ok. Give it to me straight, Pan. If we figure out a way to do this thing, what's the worst that can happen?"

"Total … world … annihilation." I deadpanned as I sipped my Negroni cocktail. "I'm half kidding. The worst that can happen is that you completely fuck up your marriage and instead of three people in your bed, there's just one: you."

"Yeah, that's not an option. I don't want to throw out my marriage just so I can have this fantasy that may not even be so great anyway. So how in the hell do people do this?" The underlying panic was showing on Claudine's face.

"Successfully? They're usually single or they are after they've done it." I smirked "And actually, it can be pretty damn great. I have tasted of the elixir of life a few times, but each situation started and ended differently. It depends on what you're both really looking for with this."

"What do you mean 'looking for'; isn't it always looking to experience something different in your sex life?"

"Yeah, sure it is, if you think you'll just do it one time and your curiosity is satisfied: the end. What happens after you've had a third party come between the two of you, and I mean that literally? Will you ever really be happy with just having your one partner back again or will you find yourself missing that extra vagina and start making this a more regular thing? There's also the detail of how you'll pick this third person and the logistics of where this is going to play out."

"See Pan, this is why I called you! Anybody else would have said holy shit, and that would be the extent of the discussion. You hear the situation and in seconds, you start to break it down and design a battle plan."

The waiter arrived with our food and about half way through our linguini with calm sauce, she encouraged me to just brain drain the "battle plan" I was working on for her.

"Ok, you have a couple of decisions to make that are critical. One regards the person you choose to bring into your bed. It can be someone you already know. It can be a stranger that you randomly pick up. It can be a stranger that you actively seek through inquiries or ads. Or it could be a professional that you hire. And don't scoff at that one. It might be your best option but let's break down the others."

"If you choose someone you know, that means that if it doesn't work out, you will have to run into them wherever you always ran into them before. Or you could move to Montana to avoid them. If it does "work out", you will have to decide if you want to do it again or just be happy that it happened once and part as friends."

"Here's the first monkey wrench; it's not uncommon after a threesome, that one of you could become very attached to the newcomer. God, I love the unintentional dirtiness of language! I digress. I'm telling you this from experience. When one in the couple falls in love with the third party, they'll try and arrange private dates with them to continue having sex and that means one of you is left home alone, maybe forever. And, Eros forbid, when the play partner falls in love with half of a couple, you can have yourself a first class stalker-loony tunes situation if the couple tries to break up with her, or him. Not a pretty picture."

"Jeesuz. I'd never have expected that!"

"Yeah well, nobody ever expects the Spanish Inquisition."

"Huh?"

"It's a Monty Python reference. Never mind." I ordered another round of drinks and we went back to eating our entrées. After a few minutes of Claudine trying to process all this information, she looked back up at me.

"So, Pan, what happened with your stalker thing and, if I may ask, how many of these triangular arrangements have you been part of?"

"I've had a few. And yes, that happened. A few years back, I had what was supposed to be a one-time sex date with a very hot woman while her husband watched. It was gloriously delicious and it was all copasetic until she started calling me when her husband wasn't home and asking if I'd come over or meet her somewhere and then the gifts started to arrive at my door. I really had to draw a hard line and cut her off or it would have not only ruined her marriage, but I had no desire for an ongoing relationship. It was very awkward. "

"Now the other ménage a trios … was pretty damn perfect. First, we three knew each other through work situations and none of us were previously involved with the others, so there wasn't any horning in on an established relationship. That was the key to our success. We just wanted to spend some time together, exploring each other. We spent two dreamy months on a boat sailing around the islands of Italy, getting tan and getting laid and at the end of the summer, we kissed goodbye and all went our separate ways. That was a slice of heaven. "

"Pandora, if you ever decide to write a memoir book, I'll be first in line to buy it just so I can live your life vicariously."

I laughed and told her not hold her breath. Perhaps when I was older and most of the lovers I've had were ancient history, maybe then, I'd think about it.

"Ok, so if you were me and you still wanted to do this thing, what would you do?" She pressed me for an answer.

"Well, you don't have kids and in this case, that's a big plus because you never want to inadvertently drag a kid through anything more confusing than the regular crap they'll go through just living their lives. I would pick another town that's just far enough away so you aren't going to run into your third person while you're in the produce aisle at the Ralph's on Wilshire. Try San Francisco or San Diego. Get copies of their local papers and read the personals to see if anyone is looking for a couple like you two. Or you can put your own ad in those papers and when you get calls, you can set up a meeting at a restaurant to see if you want to go through with this. Book a nice hotel and if all goes well, you'll be playing twister that evening. The other option is to go to Nevada and hire a professional to pop your threesome cherries and you'll never have to worry about any of the other complications. It's a simple and elegant solution."

"Brilliant! That would work and I like the idea of it being someone neither of us knows. If Jack had the hots for some babe and we brought her home, I might start to feel like his second choice. And he would probably feel the same if I brought someone in that way too."

"Claud, there's one more monkey wrench I need to warn you about."

"I'm all ears. Shoot"

"If this is going to be your first time having sex with another woman, you might find that you like it … a lot. Jack already knows he likes sex with women, but for you, this experience can awaken a sleeping dragoness inside you. You could very easily find that trying to go back to just you and Jack won't be enough anymore. I'm not kidding. "

"There probably isn't a guy alive who doesn't fantasize about having sex with two women but they never take into account that they could become a third wheel when the women continue their own party after he's passed out from exhaustion. It's really only in the porn movies where the girls are happy to just service the guy the whole time and then go back to their corners after he comes."

"In real life, when he tags out, the girls keep going and they may not miss his contribution when they're really into it. There are a whole lot of very interesting ways that women can make each other orgasm and they don't need a male to do it. Guys don't count on that because their heads are too filled with images of sugar plum pussies and two girls giving him a blow job at the same time. I'm dead serious about this, Claud. It happens and it's hard to recover your relationship when your partner is forever wondering if they're enough for you anymore. "

"It could be like a heroin addiction for you if you decide that pussy is your thing. You'd have to choose a different lifestyle or make sure Jack is happy being sidelined when you're not in the mood for cock. You might start sneaking around and lying to Jack about being at a book club or visiting your sick aunt when you're really setting up a rendezvous with a steaming bowl of red hot vagina."

Now that she was armed with some information beyond the fantasy fun of bringing a third person into a marriage bed, Claudine had her face in her hands and she was staring into the future weighing the cost of this experiment. I wondered what her final decision would be. She took a deep breath and looked up at me. "Fucking A, Pan. I'm gonna need another drink."

"I think I could fall madly in bed with you."

Author Unknown

Chapter 20

London 1988

Masquerade

She picked up on the third ring. "Diane, tell me you're not doing anything two weekends from now and that you will be coming along with me wherever I take you."

"Pandora, dear, I am free two weekends from now and I'll go with you anywhere you want to take me."

"That's why I love you. Here's the checklist: passport, city and party clothes for four days. I'm picking you up at two today to run an errand for a few hours. Deal?"

"I'm all yours. See you at two." We hung up.

Diane had played along and not asked where we were headed during our drive from her house in Huntington Beach, but now we were turning into an old warehouse district in Los Angeles and her facial expressions showed some skepticism in my location choice for a fun afternoon.

I grabbed her hand and pulled her out of the car when she hesitated. "Trust me. Besides, I have a gun if this goes down wrong." Her jaw dropped as she reluctantly got to her feet and followed me.

Malika greeted us at the door of the plain brick building that looked exactly like all the other plain brick buildings in the area. "You made good time. Come on in."

"Do you really have a gun?" she whispered as we entered and I gave her my best sarcastic bitch face.

I made the introductions and Malika led the way past the offices and loading dock and out to an enormous space that was filled with crates, boxes and hundreds of racks of clothing; each bagged and marked with an inventory tag.

"Where would you like to start Pan? We've got renaissance, pirates, vampires, super heroes, Elizabethan, Greeks and Romans, you name it and we probably have it."

"Have what?" Diane was really confused now.

"Our costumes, babe. This is a movie wardrobe warehouse and we're borrowing something to wear for a masked ball, in London, where *you* will be my guest."

"What?" She laughed loud and grabbed me to join her in jumping up and down like fifteen year olds. "That is the most amazing thing I have ever heard. Pan, I'm telling you, if I were into women, I would fuck you right now, on the floor. "She planted a big kiss on my cheek.

Malika's eyes flew wide. "She's very enthusiastic." I said by way of explanation. "Di, take a breath and close your eyes and try to picture yourself in a costume so we can figure out where to start looking."

"I'm thinking something flow-y and plunge-y. What would that be?"

"Actually, you would make a stunning Aphrodite. Come on, let's start in Greeks and Romans and see what we have." Malika headed off at a fast clip into the rows of racks and we had to move it to keep up with her.

After trying on several different styles, Diane stepped out of the dressing room wearing a gold lame toga that hit her about mid calf with a slit up to her hip and a neckline that met the heavy gold belt at her waist. Her shoes were gold sandals with wraps that crisscrossed up the leg and tied near the knee. The color was perfect with her golden blonde hair and she knew there wouldn't be a better costume for her than this one.

I had opted for an 18th century gown, with a front split and lace underskirts, and the sort of lace corset bodice that heaves your bosoms into the stratosphere.

"Do you want the hoop pannier for underneath it?" Malika had pulled all the accessories out that went with the black gown. "Oh God, no, I don't think so. I'd like to be able to move around in this. Besides, I have no plans to serve hors d'oeuvres off the shelf on my ass, so let's leave that in the box."

She handed us our zipped garment bags for the trip as we thanked her for the help and the costume loan.

The invitation had come through a musician friend and, it seemed, his party planner had reserved a small castle outside London for the event. Word was that the parties could get a little wild and none of the larger hotels in the city were too keen to open their venues again after the last crazy gathering had evolved into something close to Caligula light. The 350 guests would include luminaries from the music and film world, magazine people, record execs and the prerequisite fashion model eye candy for photo opportunities.

It doesn't take much to convince people to have a party, but when you tie the event to a worthy cause, everyone feels better about the drunken debauchery that usually goes along with celebrities and alcohol. This event would be raising funds for a private project Evan was working on, building water systems and storage tanks for villages in Burkina Faso that were in dire need. Other organizations had donated money and equipment, but without engineers to actually assemble the machines and mechanics to repair the donated trucks, villages all over Africa have rusting pieces of good intentions sitting unused and the potable water is still a two hour walk through some dangerous territory. This group was bringing equipment but also setting up a rotation series of engineers and interns to make sure locals were trained properly and everything was up and running before they headed back to their own country and their refrigerators filled with Perrier bottles.

Diane was animated and her energy was high as we boarded our plane. "I've never been to one of these before. A Halloween party, certainly, but not an official masquerade ball. I'm excited!"

We were tucked into our first class seats on a British Airways flight from LAX to Heathrow and Diane had her sleep mask pushed up on her forehead while she sipped her champagne cocktail. I was thumbing through a magazine while we waited for our dinners to be served on our ten hour flight.

She touched her sleep mask. "Hey! I can't believe it. We forgot to get masks with our costumes! Can we find something in London?"

"We're all taken care of. Remember Jennifer, the one that makes costumes for movies? I showed her what we were wearing and she made us a couple of special masks. I had them shipped directly to the hotel so they'll be there with the costumes tomorrow. "

She squeezed my arm and wriggled her body in the chair. "Oooooo. You just thought of everything! You might be the best date I've ever had!" She settled back down for a while listening to music on her headphones.

After dinner had been cleared, we rummaged through the complimentary amenity bag each first class passenger receives. We were dabbing a bit of the D.R. Harris Freshening Cologne onto wrists, rubbing the milk cucumber & roses hand lotion into our skin and pressing the warm moist towels to our faces. I had accumulated a ridiculous number of frequent flyer miles, so I used some of them to upgrade us and make this whole British adventure an even more memorable trip. With our sleep masks ready to lower and smelling like a perfume shop, we had a soft giggle fit and finally gave it up and got some sleep. "Go to sleep, damn it."

"I will if you shut up and let me."

"You're still talking" Arm slap. Return arm slap. Giggle.

The car service met us at Heathrow and took us to the Mayfair where we would be staying as well as several other party guests flying in from other places. Since it was mid morning when we arrived and dropped off our luggage, we decided to spend the day wandering through London. I pulled her into Rigby & Peller where we both bought too many bits of delicious lingerie and stockings.

By the time we got back to the room with our black shopping totes in tow, our package from the states had been delivered and Diane wanted to see what sort of masks we had.

Jennifer had outdone herself. Diane had chosen the Aphrodite costume and her mask was overlapping gold leaves that fit smoothly around the sides of her head.

Jennifer had dusted the leaves with an iridescent glitter so the mask shimmered when she turned her head from side to side.

For my black costume, she had made me an amazing monarch butterfly mask and the wings reached up to my forehead with the lower portion brushing my cheeks. She had put a few containers of shimmering eye shadows in with the masks in gold and copper and pearlized white. A consummate professional, she was one step ahead of our needs.

Jet lag had hit us both and we opted for a bottle of wine, a room service meal and a long sleep instead of hitting the local spots that evening. By morning, there was an envelope under our door along with a London Times and two red roses. I brought them inside and rang up room service for some tea.

My name was written in calligraphy on the cream envelope and when I opened it and pulled out the card, a hand full of glitter and tiny metallic cutouts of penises and breasts came along with it and floated down to the floor. **"Welcome to London My Darling Revelers! Join me tonight at my flat for welcome cocktails and other fuckery. Cheers, E,"** He always was a flamboyant soul and I could see he was going to be in fine form this weekend.

"Are these tiny penises on the floor?" Diane was wrapped in a bathrobe running a comb through her wet hair when she had stepped into the glitter and now, seated in a chair, she was peeling the tiny cocks off her feet.

"Yes they are. Get used to it and let the games begin. We've got a cocktail party tonight at Evan's" I handed her the note I'd just read.

" '… other fuckery.' I love this guy."

We arrived at Evan's around 8 p.m. and there were twenty or so others already lounging on chairs or milling around the spacious apartment while introductions were made and old friends greeted each other. Diane liked Evan immediately and within an hour, they had bonded over their mutual wicked humor and their love of shoes and all things Chanel.

When a friend of his arrived, he grabbed Diane and dragged her over to introduce them. "Jonathon, this is my new friend, Diane. You two should talk or fuck or talk and then fuck. Trust me. It'll be magical." He was swept off by another of his guests leaving Diane and Jonathon to fend for themselves for finding food and drink.

I could see that they actually did have some chemistry together so I made myself scarce. On the back patio, I found a table of people I knew from a magazine I frequently write for. Tom, the Editor in Chief, got up and found another chair and made me sit with them and fill them in on my latest projects and we caught up on office gossip.

Across the table, Leyton was engrossed in a production conversation with one of their creative directors. I had worked with him several times on concept and layout issues for photos and copy I had sold their publication. I wasn't really sure about his private story as we only ever talked about work, so for all I knew, he could have been married with a dozen children, or gay, or gay and married with a dozen children. He was a soft spoken, polite and highly intelligent man and he had that disheveled handsomeness that goes un-noticed unless you really pay attention. I'd always thought he was all kinds of delicious and it would have been very alright with me if he'd asked me to dinner but over the six years I'd known him, no invitation was forthcoming. I had long since let the possibility go.

A few people wandered away from the table leaving a chair open on one side of me and Leyton rose from where he was and carried his beer over to join me, kissing both my cheeks before he sat down. "Well, hello there stranger. I had no idea you'd be in London or that you even knew our illustrious host."

"Hi, Leyton. Good to see you. Ah, Evan and I go way back. I met him doing some music photography and we just hit it off and we've stayed in touch. Are you going to the Masque tomorrow night?"

"Perhaps. Aren't we supposed to be incognito?"

"You're probably right about that. Though I'm always laughing through movies where a pair of glasses or a little fabric over their eyes can fool a woman who is supposedly in love with the day time version of the superhero. If a woman can't recognize a man's lips or his hair or his eyes and lashes, and for God's sake, if she doesn't know the cut of his shoulders or the curve of his ass when he's walking away, then she never really looked at him in the first place. You know what I mean?"

"Yes, I do. And I can only hope that there's a woman out there who has paid that sort of close attention to me and the curve of my ass at some time."

"Leyton, I would recognize your ass anywhere."

"Really? Well, Ms. Bleue. I'm shocked. I'm also forever grateful for the lovely rise I just got out of that revelation. "

"Flirty? Well, here's a side of you I've never seen. I like it!"

"Pandora, I don't believe we've actually ever seen each other outside of a boardroom or away from a production table, even after all these years."

I was taken aback at that insight. He was right. We hadn't even had a lunch at a restaurant outside the magazine offices since all our working meals had been catered in to allow us to continue our meetings.

"You're absolutely right! I've never thought about that. You know, Leyton, I don't even know if you're married or whatever. Tell me about yourself."

"First, I am not married and not currently 'whatever'. I'm very much single. I grew up in the Cotswold's. I went to University at Oxford and obtained my master's degree from Yale. I am not a vegetarian. I smoke the occasional cigarette when I'm feeling a bit Hemingway. I am a secret Science Fiction fan, a Chelsea Football fanatic and I happen to think that Clint Eastwood is an overrated actor and no matter what the character calls for, he plays them all exactly the same, ad nausea."

I was laughing by the time he'd made it half way through his quirky bio and found myself even more charmed by him then I'd been before. We were lured into a wider conversation going on at the table and then back into the main house where more guests had arrived.

Throughout the evening we would pass each other heading to food areas or off to chat with someone. Each time we passed, we would find a way to touch an arm or make some small physical connection and smile. There was some electricity here worth investigating.

Diane and Jonathon were sitting close together on a sofa. She had taken off her heels and had her legs tucked under her and they were deep in their own conversation.

I was watching them for a moment when Evan came up behind me and rested his head on my shoulder to watch along with me.

"See? I'm a fucking genius when it comes to coupling others. Mark my words; they'll be doing the deed before this weekend's over. My work here is done." He squeezed me tightly and kissed my cheek before he wandered off to a guest who was waving him over.

About 2 am, Diane whispered to me that she would be in Jonathon's room at the same hotel where we were staying and she would see me in the morning. Evan had arranged for limos to leave the hotel at 5pm for the drive out to the castle so there was plenty of time for play and to get ready for the ball. I gave her a hug and found a small group of people who were also heading back and we shared a taxi. I welcomed the quiet and comfort of the luxurious bed in our room.

After a wonderful sleep, I was showered, wrapped in the thick robe the hotel provided and reading the paper when Diane tip-toed in on her walk of shame holding her heels in hand, still in her red cocktail dress with barely managed sex hair. "Oh, thank God you're awake. My legs are still wobbly and I need some coffee desperately. Are you drinking tea? "

"Nope. It's imported Illy coffee. It's addicting. Park your rear and I'll pour for you."

"You're an angel. Just pour it right into my eyes." As I filled her cup, she reached to my plate and snatched my chocolate croissant and took a large bite. "I'm starving! Jesus, I think I lost ten pounds last night."

"Really? How'd you manage that?"

"He pulled out."

I roared with laughter.

The day was a lazy blur of talking and primping for the event that night. A talented painter in her own right, Diane had offered to do my makeup for me and created dramatic gold and copper eyes lined in kohl black to go with my butterfly mask. From her suitcase, she surprised me by producing several clip in sections of hair in my color. After she'd curled and fluffed to perfection, she clipped the sections in amongst my own hair giving me an impossible amount of massive waves reaching down my back.

She had painted her face in more subtle tones but also lined her light blue eyes in dramatic black, but her dress and her daring cleavage were the main highlight of her party look. Carefully placing body tape on the sides of her breasts so her cleavage would be prominent in the plunge of the gold lame Aphrodite costume, she rouged her nipples so when they did stray into view, they would look "freshly sucked" as she explained.

She made me rouge mine as well and after we were clothed, perfumed and masked, we headed to the lobby to catch the limo ride to the castle with other guests who were also waiting there.

Jonathon was already in the lobby, sitting in a wing chair with a drink in hand. He saw Diane when the elevator doors opened and he rose from his chair, drawing in a breath when he saw her looking all golden and glorious in her costume. He had chosen to wear a 19th century gentleman's long jacket and pants, a white shirt with cloth tie and black boots and looked quite dashing as he held out his arm to escort Diane to the waiting car. If the costumes here in the lobby were a preview of the others at this event, there would be some fantastic images that I hoped someone would be capturing on film.

The drive out took us through city and into countryside to the castle. Evan's party planner had lined the long drive with lanterns to light the way and there were footmen waiting at the main entrance to open doors and help the guests from the limos.

Inside there were enormous floral arrangements and a string quartet in the large ballroom playing Baroque pieces. Buffet tables were laden with enough food to feed a small island nation and, of course, over the top displays of pheasants and suckling pig complete with an apple in its mouth. The yards of beautiful fruits and sweets made the scene look as if Renoir himself had arranged it this evening for a new still life painting.

Evan swept into the room to applause as the guests poured in from outside gardens and other rooms where they had wandered off to tour the castle and grounds. When he had our attention he greeted us all and thanked us for attending. He pointed to a crystal bowl on the largest fireplace mantle and told us that if we wanted to make a money contribution for his water project, we could leave our checks in the bowl and that was all the business that he was going to mention.

"I have a special treat for any who wishes to partake." Servers entered the room carrying trays with what appeared to be rose petals on them and began to circulate amongst the guests. "The roses have a very special 'sugar' (he used air quotes), my own recipe, and if you'd like to fly with angels tonight, join me! Let the fuckery begin!" He gave a dramatic hand flourish and bow and took a rose petal from a passing silver tray and popped it into his mouth.

I was feeling very adventurous, and no doubt braver by far in the semi anonymity of the costume and mask, which is certainly the whole point of a night like this; to create an atmosphere where you can be someone else for a little while. Diane and Jonathon had already taken their rose petals and Evan arrived at my side as the server came near me with another tray full.

"It's a new drug called Ecstasy, darling. I had my cook crush it and mix it with sugar for the candied rose petals. Just a light dose. Nothing too heavy. Genius. Don't you think? "

"You're very clever, Evan, as usual. This isn't going to make me hallucinate my ass off like the night you brought me to The Reactions concert and fed me the magic mushrooms, is it?"

"No, love, this is going to make you want to spread your wings and kiss the sky. You'll be fine. I promise." I took a rose petal and with a "cheers mate", I put it on my tongue.

I milled around the party chatting with people as I went and half an hour later, I was starting to feel a very slight buzz across the surface of my skin and a smile was hovering on my lips as the room began to take on a dreamy and beautiful movie set atmosphere.

From across the way, a man I hadn't seen yet that evening was watching me. He was dressed in a classic Zorro costume, complete with sword, hat, whip and a cape that was covering his black clothing. Certainly, the rose petal catalyst was enhancing the view, but I thought he looked sexy as hell.

The smile that I couldn't control anymore spread across my face and he turned his back, swept his cape aside and gestured dramatically with his gloved hand to his ass. Leyton! Fabulous!

I'm not sure if I walked over to where he was or floated. By the look in his eyes and the same uncontrollable smile that I wore, it appeared he'd taken a rose petal as well. He put out his arm for me to take and when I laced mine through his, he swiftly led me out of the room and down a hall way with some destination in mind.

I was feeling all sorts of wonderful shivers over my skin and for someone who talks as much as I do, there wasn't anything to say at that particular time, so I just went along with feeling.

When we arrived at a heavy carved oak door, he opened it and led me into what I could see was a private library. He locked the door behind him and he moved swiftly to me and reaching to the front slit of my dress, he moved the lace underskirt away and grabbed me around my hips and carried me back to the desk sitting me on its edge.

My body was humming from head to toe from the petals and from Leytons surprising authority in the moment. I was beyond turned on by this version of the man with whom I had only previously shared highlighter pens and sticky notes. He unlaced the bodice of my dress and pulled me up, letting it fall to the floor at my feet. Picking it up and tossing it over a chair he turned to me and I was standing now in front of him in the black satin Basque, stockings and a lacey g-string that barely skimmed my pubic bones.

He pulled me towards him and crushed his mouth to mine and kissed again at the very apex of my cleavage. He reached for my g-string and moved it quickly down my legs and I sat back on the desk so he could free it from my high heels.

Unzipping his pants, Leyton let them fall and having been ready for me for some time now, he pushed his legs between mine. Reaching under both my thighs he lifted my legs onto his shoulders and he slid his hard cock into me. I braced my hands behind me on the desk as I dropped my head back and moaned out loud at the fantastic sensation of him inside me. He held me up that way for several minutes as he ground his hips and pumped me senseless until he came.

Leyton/Zorro, reached for a fountain pen from the desk blotter behind me and with it, he wrote a large "Z" on the full round of my right breast, laughing as he did it. He zipped back into his pants, kissed my mouth again and with a Hollywood whirl of his cape, he left out the door.

I found a small restroom off the library and pulled myself together, stepping back into my dress and rejoined the party hoping to find Zorro for another duel later.

There would be three more encounters with Leyton during the party; one, fully dressed, from behind with my skirts hiked up on my back, then an orgasm, mine, delivered by his hand hidden in the folds of my skirt while we danced in the ballroom. I then returned the favor with my hand through his unzipped pants beneath his cape as we leaned on a wall in the shadows of the garden. I had produced a tube of my red lipstick and placed a "P" on his neck, just below his ear, marking him as he had done to me.

On the plane heading back to Los Angeles a few days later, Diane was dreamy eyed as she ran her finger around her champagne glass rim.

"Thinking about Jonathon, are you?"

"Yes. I'm completely smitten. He's coming to L.A. next month and we'll have a whole week together. "

"Don't you have a date with Nigel tomorrow night?" I asked, having remembered the film premier she had promised to attend with her sometimes companion.

"I canceled. I can't go, Pan. It just feels like leaving Le Cirque after having the best meal you've ever had in your life and with the flavor still on your tongue, stopping at a street vendor for a chili dog."

"Got it. You two are very good medicine together, Di."

"So, what about Zorro? Do you think that might be going anywhere?"

"He's delicious. That's for certain. I'm fairly sure at this point in my life that I just might be a lone wolf. I do know though, that I now have a perfect collection of play mates and they'll keep me very, very busy for a long, long time."

"I have found men who didn't know how to kiss. I've always found the time to teach them."

Mae West

Chapter 21

Kowloon, Hong Kong 1990

Savoring the Petals

He was in the Bridal Tea House on Arthur Street again and this time, he wasn't pretending to read the menu anymore. He looked towards me and gave a slow and stunning smile and I nodded a brief acknowledgement. I had been here in Kowloon for the past two weeks, gathering photos for an article on jade for a magazine that I occasionally do freelance work for.

My days had been spent wandering the small shops and winding roads throughout Hong Kong, taking meetings with local gemologists and cultural anthropologists at the Hong Kong Heritage Museum. My notebooks were filled with research and I'd even purchased a few interesting jade pieces for myself as their beauty was enhanced by learning more about its place in Chinese cultural history.

I finished my Keemun tea and left out the door heading south towards Win Sing Lane, to leisurely make my way back to the Hyatt, where I was staying. Small shops along the way drew me in with their fascinating window displays, but on this day, I found myself drawn into an antiques shop tucked on a small side street.

The shop was filled with porcelain vases, beautifully painted lacquer boxes, intricately carved jade standing art and the pieces that had caught my eye from the sidewalk; the antique map collection. I was completely engrossed by the scrolled and flat maps that covered several tables. Here were land and nautical maps of China and the South Pacific, listing places whose names had changed half a dozen times since the 1700's when the cartographer had drawn them. They were wonderful pieces and the perfect gift for my editor, who had a large collection of antique and contemporary maps framed on his office walls.

While sifting through the stacks, making a selection of one for myself and another for the gift, a hand came down with a branch of purple orchids and set them on top of the maps. I looked up to see the man from the tea shop was standing next to me.

"Beauty for beauty," he said. I smiled and picked up the flower branch and turned back to hear what this stranger would say next. I had seen him four other times either in the tea shop or on the street nearby and I'd wanted to photograph his classic Chinese image. He was several inches taller than me and he wore a black Mandarin collared casual business suit with a white collarless shirt beneath it. His handsome face and easy smile was framed with jet black hair, and almond shaped eyes of a dark mahogany brown.

"I have seen you for many days. This, I bring to you." He pointed at the flower.

"Xie xie. They're very beautiful." I pressed my hands together and gave a small bow of my head as I spoke. "I know only a little Mandarin, I am sorry about that. Um … Ni jiao shen me ming zi? Your name?" I said it very slowly and I'm sure I butchered the pronunciation but he appeared to be pleased at my effort.

"I am Yusheng. And you?"

"I am Pandora … um … Pan."

"Pan. Yes." He extended his hand and when I placed mine in his, he added his other hand to cover mine and softly said my name again.

"You are a visitor?"

"Yes, a visitor. I live in California and I'm working in Hong Kong for a few more days."

His presence was soft in the way that a tiger might have soft fur. It seemed like there could be an abundance of coiled power moving smoothly beneath the loose drape of his clothing and I could sense a keen interest and a level of heat in the way he was looking at me.

"You can come with me to see the city?" He wanted to spend time with me and I was curious just who this stranger was. While he had been looking at me this week, I had also been looking at him and I wanted to hear his story. I accepted his offer and explained that I had to make my purchases and then I could go along on his tour and he told me he would wait.

After completing the purchase and customs forms so the maps could be shipped directly to my home, I joined him by the door and he held it open as we made our way onto Nathan Road.

We walked and he asked me about the work I was do-ing and I explained about the jade story. Smiling, he told me that his name, in Mandarin, means Jade Birth. I shared that I had learned jade was considered the stone of heaven in Chinese culture. He told me about jade's embodiment of both yin and yang in the world, as well as it being the connection between heaven and earth, or the physical and the spiritual worlds.

I asked if his name had influenced the way he lived his life and he said that through his art, he endeavored to bring the beauty of the heavens to the physical world through his canvases, so yes, it had served as a compass for his career choice. He asked more about what sort of photography and writing I had done and said he wanted to understand the spirit of what I have brought to the world. I'd never heard it put quite that eloquently before and with a stroke of serendipity, we were approaching a block where I knew a bookstore had some of my work for sale. I had signed some copies for them just a week prior.

I said if he wanted, I could show him, and he followed me to the bookstore. I greeted the owner who smiled and bowed waving us towards the book section where she had prominently displayed my work on a table top with a small poster announcing signed copies for sale. We found some chairs and I told him to sit and brought him over a few books. Not wanting to launch right into the work I'd done of a more erotic nature, I first gave him the book with my portrait collection of some famous faces and others I had selected for their interesting looks.

He turned the pages slowly, taking in the images and nodding as he went, sometimes with a comment on the light sources I had used or the way a head was tilted or an expression I had preserved in a candid moment.

He spent some time on the collection of erotic images in the next book; close up shots of curves along a body or contact between two people in various acts. He moved his hand in the air like he was painting or conducting an orchestra and said he found the flowing motion of the images hypnotic.

Finally, I gave him the Horimono book and he was engrossed in the images of the full body tattoo work. He spent the most time studying the photos of Sakura, the Geisha Girl with the cherry blossom tree covering her body. He studied them closely and then stood suddenly and taking my hand, pulled me from the store saying "Come. I must show you my work."

We walked a few blocks over and he pulled open the door of a contemporary gallery that featured the work of several Chinese artists. He waved to the owner and continued, pulling me behind with a singular purpose. There on the white gallery walls, hung a collection of eight paintings of women that were part of his newest series. They were about 40" X 60" each and their subjects were different women lying nude across a flat surface and their bodies were covered in flower blossoms from the tips of their toes all the way up and even scattered throughout their hair. Each blossom girl wore a uniquely different bloom that he felt had suited their spirit.

I was knocked out at the beauty of these pieces. Their innocence and eroticism was perfectly balanced with the surreal nature of the images, falling into that middle world between fantasy and reality. I shared my thoughts with Yusheng and he smiled and said that is the way of jade; to be the guide to the place where heaven and earth merge together through his brush. He was very pleased that I had seen that so quickly in his work.

We made our way back down the main road and he brought me to a noodle shop where we talked further about our individual styles of artistic expression. He liked that I was comfortable with my chop sticks. He said they make you take your time. Then he said so many from the West come to China and instead of slipping into the soft walk here, they clomp in with hard shoes, demanding forks so they can grab more food, more quickly and hurry out the door again. He said that his was an old and patient world and that perhaps, in our hurrying and gathering of all the things we think we must have, we miss the thousand things that wait quietly in beauty, for us to slow down and find them.

He walked me back to the Hyatt Tsim Sha Tsui on Hanoi Street and to the elevator bank off the lobby. Yusheng pulled me aside to a private spot around the corner. He put his hand on the side of my face and with a caress ran it down my neck and to my breast and with a firm but gentle pressure there, he ran his hand back up to my face again and pulled me towards him for a kiss. "I must paint you, Pan. Please? Will you come to my studio tomorrow and let me paint you so I do not lose this?"

It was a surprising request. I am the one behind the camera, not in front, and the only time anyone had every drawn me was when I did a brief stint as a life art model in my late teens. I was flattered and intrigued and frankly, honored having seen the quality of his artwork in the gallery that day.

"It would be my honor, Yusheng." He gave me a radiant smile and dug through his pocket for a pen and notepad to write his studio address and instructions for the taxi driver the next day.

He kissed me once again. "Until then Pan, my eyes and my heart will be filled with you." He turned and headed back out into the noise of the city and I half floated, still carrying my purple orchid branch up the elevator and to my room.

As he requested, I hailed a cab, early in the morning and handed the directions to the driver who said the ride to the studio would be about thirty minutes. I settled into my seat and watched the morning unfolding as we inched our way through city traffic and out to the Cross Harbour Tunnel and beyond to Hong Kong Island.

The sight of modern skyscrapers covered in the precarious looking bamboo scaffolding that crawled up twenty stories high, bearing the weight of construction crews and equipment, is a contrast we would never see in the U.S.A. The thought of using bamboo poles on a glass and steel building site would have our safety inspectors stroking out, yet here, in this ancient city, it's just another day to the welder sending sparks into the air from his perch high up in the Hong Kong skyline.

I paid the driver and stepped out of the car and up to the red door of Yusheng's two story studio on the Peak. The bell gave a chirring sound and in a moment, he was there, welcoming me in. His feet were bare and he wore a pair of jeans that had probably been broken in ten years earlier. They displayed a splattering of a dozen colors and the brown t-shirt he wore had the same evidence of his enthusiasm for his painting.

"Please, come in, Pan. I have made tea and I also have some food if you would like something to eat before we get started. " I followed him down a short hallway and to the back of the building where the ceiling opened up to the second floor giving the room a vast feeling and a frame for the wall of windows letting light in from the unbroken view of the harbor. Turning back, I could see that where I had entered was still a two floor structure and up the spiral staircase, I assumed would be an office, a bathroom and possibly a bedroom if he found himself working late and stayed here through the night.

We drank our tea and he showed me some of the rough sketches he was working on for the next series after he completed the Blossom work. I asked how many more Blossoms he would be doing and he said he had just one more. "You." I flushed and shook my head at this admission. "Really? Yusheng, I am... beyond moved. Thank you."

When we were ready, he brought me over to the area where I would be posing and showed me the narrow bed-like surface, covered with white fabric and set against a tall white backdrop. No other color would be in the space but what I would be bringing and whatever else he was adding. He had a privacy screen and let me go and change for the sitting. I had brought along a lovely silk robe that I'd found on this trip and I slipped out of my clothes and pulled it around me and made my way back out to the set.

He had brought a very large wicker basket into the room and a small white rolled neck pillow. "I need you here, please, on your back, this direction." I slipped out of the robe and stepped to the bed and lay down where he had indicated. He drew in a breath and released it slowly as he watched me cross before him, naked. "Yes. This will be perfect. I work very fast, but I'd like to take a few photos for reference if you don't mind."

He had me stretch out and bent my far knee and set my foot down flat. He had me throw my left arm over my head and the right was dangling out towards his easel with my hand open and draped down towards the floor. He had a hair brush and moved my hair out where he needed it, all with feather light touches and a radiant smile on his face. He worked quietly and swiftly, having a very clear picture in his mind of what he wanted to create and eager to get to the brushes and colors waiting on his palette.

Now, he went to retrieve the wicker basket and when he opened the lid, there was a riot of color inside. He had chosen bougainvillea blossom for me. He couldn't have known they were my favorite, but there they were, hundreds of the paper-like deep fuchsia pink petals. He took many handfuls and placed them all along my body until they were softly covering me, scattered on my nipples and my vagina, even tossed on my bent knee and across my toes. The sensation was amazing and the sensual beauty of the blossoms had me smiling like a fool as he brushed his hands together and stepped back to see if he had it right.

Like many artists, he first took a few photos so that he could continue painting for as many days as it took to complete the piece. He went, then, to his easel and began to mix the pigments and his brush touched down on the gesso covered canvas to begin its transformation from white to a blaze of color. I listened to the music he had playing through the studio; an eclectic mix of classical, contemporary, rock, jazz and world music. He worked silently putting as much color on the canvas as he could before he felt I would need a break and the blossoms would fall away.

After a stretch of about 45 minutes, he asked how I was doing and I told him I was good for at least another hour. I told him I practice stillness when I'm lying in the sun for hours at a time and I was pretending I was on a beach in

Bali while he painted. His laughter had a warm sound and it made me smile again.

A bit later, he stopped and set his brush and palette down and wiped his hands on a cloth he had hanging out of his back pocket. He made his way over to the bed and knelt down next to it. Lifting a blossom that was near my lips, he bent over me and kissed my mouth with heat behind it and before I could respond, he said "No. Be still. Let me." And he made his way down my neck moving blossoms as he went and kissing what was hidden beneath them. He lifted the petal at my nipple and kissed, and sucked at it making it harden with his touch. He brushed more bougainvilleas from my belly and trailed a dozen soft kisses until he moved down and put his lips between my legs and licked the edges of my vagina. Blossoms began to slide off my body as he used his tongue to pleasure me to orgasm.

He returned to my lips then and kissed me with more heat and then put his hand out for me to rise. He handed me my robe and I knew our sitting was over, and so it seemed was the sensual interlude. I didn't question him as this day was perfect exactly as it was. After I dressed, I joined him by the canvas and saw how much of the painting he had finished. There I was looking like a dream version of who I really was. He said he would complete it in the next few days and when it was dry, it would be hung in the show we had seen the day before.

He took my face in his hands as we stood there looking at his painting and he kissed me once again. I asked if he did his other blossom sessions this way as well, and he said yes and that he never made love to the Blossoms as he wouldn't be unfaithful to his wife.

"Your wife. You're married? You never mentioned that. Does she know about your sessions here?"

"Yes, of course. She sees that this is how I come to the beauty of my work. She understands and she knows that I will never pluck the flower, only savor the flower's petals."

The momentary surprise or disappointment that had shadowed over me washed away as I heard the simple poetry of his words. Savor the petals. I understood that, as well. It was like the chopstick conversation we had at the noodle shop. "In our hurrying and gathering of all the things we think we must have, we miss the thousand things that wait quietly in beauty, for us to slow down and find them."

Yes. Savor the petals.

The day before I left Hong Kong, I wandered back to the gallery. Yusheng had sent me a gift at my hotel with a note letting me know the painting was hanging now. The note had arrived along with a silk fabric covered box containing a pair of silver chopsticks and bougainvillea blooms tied onto it. Here in this gallery, half a world away from my home, hanging on the wall with all the other Blossoms, was my painting. The riot of color from the blossoms made me look like a lusty nature spirit. A sense of wonder filled me as I realized that this painting would one day hang on a wall of a collector and they would never know that it was me beneath the bougainvillea petals.

"To have her here in bed with me, breathing on me, her hair in my mouth – I count that as something of a miracle."

Henry Miller

Chapter 22

Chicago 2011

Time in a Bottle

I pushed the sleeve of my cashmere turtle neck dress up my arm and sprayed a bit of Balenciaga Paris perfume onto my wrist. I closed my eyes and inhaled the fragrance to see if I wanted to buy it.

"I always preferred you wearing this one."

My eyes flew open and there was Benjamin holding a bottle of Joy de Patou at the tips of his fingers and smiling at me like a fool.

"Benjamin! Good God. What a surprise! What's it been, thirty five years?"

He stepped towards me and gave me a hug. "It may be. Do you live in Chicago now?"

"No, I'm just here for a business thing and I had the afternoon free, so, shopping the Mag Mile was a must do. How about you? Do you live here now?"

"No, we're in New York but I'm here for a one day meeting. Heading back to O'Hare in about..." he was looking at his watch now. A Breguet, I had noticed. Nice.

Expensive. "… oh …three hours" he said."My God, it's good to see you, Pandora. Let me look at you."

He took my hands and made a small step back and ran those eyes from top to bottom, taking in my dress, the leather belt at my waist that matched the boots, and he turned my hand to look for a ring.

"You are still beautiful. And I see no ring here. How is it that some lucky guy hasn't tied the knot with you?

"Wow, what is it with you and ropes?" I couldn't resist and he gave a rich rolling laugh in response.

With a shake of his head he said my name. "Pan, Pan, Pan. What would you say to a drink someplace where we can sit down and visit for while before I have to go?"

"I'd say that sounds divine. Give me twenty minutes to finish here and I'll meet you over at the door. Spiaggia is just up the street if that works for you?"

"Perfect. Twenty it is." He wandered off to do whatever it was he had come into Neiman's for when he'd recognized me and stopped to say hello.

The cosmetics counter salesgirl, somewhere in her 20's, had gathered my purchases together and had been standing politely back to give me and Benjamin some privacy while we talked. I selected a few more items and handed them to her with the perfume I was holding. On impulse, I threw in a bottle of Joy, for old time's sake, as well.

As she rang up my order and lined the shopping bag with tissues, she looked up at me and spoke. "For an older man, he's very handsome. He looks sort of like an actor from way back that my mom had a huge crush on. I can't think of his name. Were you two, um, together?"

"If you mean, together, as in the biblical sense, then yes. We were. He was the one that drove you crazy and gave you whip lash orgasms, and then he was the one that got away."

She blushed madly and gave a nervous laugh as she handed me the bag saying, "I can see there's still some kind of spark there with you two ... you know?"

"Oh, honey, that never goes away. When you're older, you'll learn that with voltage that high, it isn't smart to stick your fingers in the socket anymore." I gave her a wink and a wave as I wandered over to the door just as Benjamin arrived with his own purchases in tow.

We made our way through the afternoon foot traffic on Michigan Ave and talked casually about his wife and his kids who were now out of college and living their own lives. His daughter was the same age I was when I was with him and he had a stricken look about him as he said it killed him to know what she might be doing with some guy out there. This was his little girl. I reminded him that thirty five years ago, I was someone's little girl too.

We had arrived at the restaurant and the maitre de seated us at a window table with a spectacular view of the street below and Oak Street Beach. Our conversation was easy and rambling as we shared our Reader's Digest versions of the past three and half decades of our lives. We laughed over some memories of moments we had together and he argued with specifics I provided when his selective amnesia had conveniently left them off.

"OK. I am thoroughly impressed with your memory for detail, Pan. You were always ready with a quote from some author or some random fact. I'll bet you're the devil to beat at trivial pursuit. These days, I can hardly remember what I had for breakfast and you can tell me exactly what I was wearing in a hotel suite on a particular night decades ago. That's very impressive."

"The memory thing is a blessing and it's a curse. But, Benjamin, what is it I've done for a living all these years? My job, my passion, is to notice all the details while life is happening and to record them in the pictures I make or in the words I write so that someone else can see them and experience the moment as well."

"Well put. Your phrasing was always eloquent. I recall just sitting back and listening when you were on a roll. How is it you didn't end up teaching at a university somewhere?" He had a thoughtful look on his face now.

"Gads! Can you actually picture me stuck in the same setting, year after year, regurgitating the same things to a bunch of hung over millennials with fake tans that make them look like they rolled in a bag of Doritos while they're texting their besties about where they're gonna hookup tonight?"

He was sitting back in his chair laughing out loud. "See? That's what I mean. Your little tirades may be long at times, but they're laced with this acerbic wit and wisdom that Dorito kids could really use. It would do them a world of good for someone like you to grab them and shake them out of their stupors. They need you, Pan. "

"Well, they will just have to soldier on without me."

I knew that it might be another thirty five years that we no longer had before another moment like this one came along to speak this honestly with him. I seized the chance to turn the conversation towards our own relationship so long ago. "So, did you *need* me Benjamin? Ever?"

"Need. That's a loaded word." He paused and took a drink before he continued. "I needed your passion. I needed your fearless grip on life. I needed the way you could make me laugh. I needed your wisdom when I'd lose my way and you could guide me back to it. I needed your body near me, and on me. I needed the way you made me feel when I was with you and I needed the way I felt when you weren't with me. You brought all the pieces of my fractured needs all together. After you, I could see that it might be possible to have someone in my life who would be willing to play, hard, but who could also make a home and a life with me."

"But it wasn't me that you did all that with, B. It wasn't me that you married." I took a breath before I spoke again. "Had you asked, I would have. You know that."

"Yes. I knew. I couldn't do that to you Pan. I couldn't tie you down. Well, not that way. Other ways, yes. (he smirked) ...but not in that way. You were too much, too vast and wild and you needed much more room to live than I was willing to give a woman if she wanted to be with me. And I'm not saying you would have cheated on me, but I'm certain, eventually, I wouldn't have been enough for you. It would have broken my heart to see that happen. You would have left me, eventually."

I was dumbfounded at his admission. All of what he said was true and I knew all along that the compromises I made for him were wearing on me. I knew full well that after he was out of my life and I had recovered my own power back, that I was happier than I'd actually been when I was with him. The constant wondering what the future might look like with him colored everything I did. When it was over, it felt like I'd just returned from a year long voyage with perpetual sea sickness and finally back on land, my stomach had settled and I could walk again.

He had a little more to say. "Pan, I knew that you could walk out my door any moment and I would never see you again. For me, having you in my life was like having a jaguar befriend me, knowing the whole time, if you'd wanted to, you could have ripped my face off or just walked back to the jungle where you came from. But for awhile, I had this jaguar and she lie down next to me and let me stroke her fur. It's the stuff that fantasies are made of. "

"Well, thank you for not using 'cougar'." We both laughed and I continued. "You know Benjamin, you were the only person that I've ever allowed to have that much control over me. The surrender was the seduction. Being the Olympic level control freak that I am, letting go and surrendering to your next whim was my Mount Everest. If I'd just given you control of the sex part with us, it would have been easier for me. Instead, I tried to hand you my heart as well and we both know how that turned out."

"Pandora, I'm so sorry for the way we ended. I handled it poorly. I know." His contrition was genuine.

"I was pretty crushed when I heard you'd gotten married so soon after we broke it off. It was confirmation to me that beneath that carefully controlled exterior, you actually did want more out of life than a garter belted woman waiting on your bed."

"Oh, I still want that," he teased. "It was the jaguar thing again. Should I have built a cage for you to make you stay? You would have suffocated and it would have killed me if I'd crushed your spirit like that. You know it's true."

"Yeah, Benjamin, I know. I found the same conclusion at the bottom of a bottle of tequila. And then I pulled it together and walked back into my life."

"If your work is any indication of the life you've had, it's been quite a good one." he offered.

"You've seen my work?"

"Of course I have. Google, babe. I'm completely wired for sound over here." He playfully tapped the iPhone he had placed on the table. "I search your name occasionally to see what you're doing now. " He looked up at me, almost shyly. "I also have all your books in my library."

"I'll be damned. Does your wife know who I am?"

He chuckled and took a big drink from his glass. "Yes, well ... funny story. Years ago, she found a pack of photos that I had in my closet."

"Oh shit. Not those photos!" I blanched.

"No, no. Pictures of you naked would have been an easier find. She already knew my appetites for images of a certain nature. No. It wasn't 'those' photos. She found a picture of me that you'd taken in the hills behind my house. It was a candid shot of just my face. She liked it so she had it enlarged and framed and kept it on our dresser."

"Oh, God. I know exactly which one you're talking about."

"I thought you might. Anyway, my famously big mouthed sister, Jan, your biggest fan by the way; saw it there on the dresser. Later, at dinner with the whole family gathered around the table, she blurted out 'isn't that picture of you, one that Pandora took?' which led to a lengthy game of Pan stories with my other siblings, who also adore you. That night, my wife took the photo down and said she'd just realized why she loved it so much. She said she understood now that whoever had taken it, they loved me and the way I was looking back at the camera, I loved them too."

"The camera never lies." I said. It's always stunning to witness the impact that an image I've created can have on others, sometimes years later.

"Yes, well. It's one thing to hear about someone your spouse was involved with and to wonder just how serious it was. It's quite another to see evidence that you can measure in Scoville units staring right at you."

"I'm sorry that happened. Also flattered that you kept the photo, but sorry that it caused a road bump." We were quiet for a few minutes, sipping our drinks as we watched the passersby on Michigan Avenue below us.

"I like this on you" He pointed to a narrow silver streak of hair that now resides at my temples.

"What, the grey?

"Yes. It suits you. You're, just, well, you're softer now."

"Was I hard before?"

"Not hard. No. That would indicate callousness and you were never that. You were tough. You always knew what you wanted and you weren't afraid to ask for it, or to receive it when it was offered. I miss that about you. There aren't many women in the world that live their lives with the same confidence that men are expected to have in theirs. It's damn sexy." He took a sip of his drink. "It's intimidating as hell, but damn sexy."

"I'm intimidating? I don't recall you ever having a problem giving me direction … in the bedroom or out."

"That was the thrill of you, Pan. Don't you see? You were so willful and so very … alive. What would be the fun in walking a horse around in circles in a paddock when you could rope and ride a wild mustang?"

"That's an interesting metaphor. I wrote something once that referenced an 'activity' of ours that involved you holding my mane and riding me just like that." I laughed wickedly into my drink.

"Ah yes. A vision of your heavenly ass and your back muscles flexing just popped into my head, and if you don't stop this line of conversation, I may be forced to pull you into the restroom right now and relieve this ache."

I laughed. "Well, Benjamin, that's not going to happen. I won't be burning my life down for you again and I won't be the carelessly tossed match that burns down the forest, roots and all, of yours."

The three hours flew by and though we knew we could carry this on for days, we took this time as the gift that it was. The chance to meet again and to talk, really talk, without the retreat to the silence and action of a bedroom where we feel so much, but sometimes, say so little.

He flagged down a taxi on Michigan Ave and as it pulled to the curb, he opened the door and leaned in to ask the driver to wait just a moment and I heard the driver say, "Sure, pal. It's your dime."

He turned back to me one last time. "You were amazing, Pandora. If I would have been just a little bit different, we would have been amazing together."

I reached the back of my hand to his face to gently brush his cheek and when our skin connected, there was a feeling of live electrical current at the touch. I know he felt it too when I saw those, still beautiful, ocean blue eyes fly wide and he took in an involuntary breath.

"I know, Benjamin. I remember. I remember everything."

"Women who love themselves are threatening; but men who love real women, are more so."

Naomi Wolf

A Final Note

Now you've heard some of the stories from my life and if you've paid attention, you'll know I'm not a child anymore. If you've felt heat during your private viewing of some fires I have lit or stood within, you'll understand a little better that the embers linger on years later.

When you see the flush of color and the knowing smile cross the face of the silver haired woman as she sees the passing lovers with wandering hands, you'll understand now, what just shadowed through her mind. And when she casts her eyes down and casually brushes her hair back, caressing her own face, you'll know she is feeling, for just one more moment, the hand of her own lover touch her cheek again.

The heat of us remains beneath whatever time and circumstance have done to our physical body. The goddess who fans our fire remains as long as we can remember her. We all burn and from our fires, the world is born. From our fires, the painters paint, the writers write and the musicians shape a tribute to the flame that once touched their skin.

We all burn; every age, every color, and every shape. We express that burning in our lives a thousand different ways; from the small flicker of a candle flame to the wildfire that leaves the landscape changed forever.

These could be your aunt's personal stories. You know, the one with the passport filled with stamps of foreign lands? These could be your mother's most private memories, hard as that may be for you to grasp. When you see the faded photos of the stranger in her collection, you will wonder now, if maybe this had been her Benjamin.

I haven't told you everything. Some memories are too intense for sharing even here. Other memories are too fragile to risk the transfer onto paper. This will have to be enough for now.

And so my little sisters, I leave you with your thoughts, now filled with possibilities. Know yourself, above all else.

Still Burning,
Pandora

"There comes a point in your life when you realize who really matters, who never did, and who always will."

Author Unknown